The Strange Adventures of Captain Dangerous

George Augustus Sala

Contents

THE STRANGE ADVENTURES OF CAPTAIN DANGEROUS

BY

George Augustus Sala

TO
ALEXANDER MUNRO,
=Sculptor=,
THIS BOOK,
IN TOKEN OF SINCERE AND ADMIRING FRIENDSHIP, IS
CORDIALLY INSCRIBED.

PREFACE.

IN the last century--and many centuries before the last; but it is about the eighteenth that I am specially speaking--long before steamers and railways, or even frigate-built ships and flying coaches were dreamt of, when an Englishman went abroad, he stopped there. When he came back, if at all, it was, as a rule, grizzled and sunburnt, his native habits all unlearnt, and his native tongue more than half forgotten. Even the Grand Tour, with all that money could purchase in the way of couriers and post-horses, to expedite matters for my Lord, his chaplain, his courier, and his dancing master, took as many years as it now does months to accomplish. There were no young novelists in those days to make a flying-trip to the Gaboon country, to ascertain whether the stories told by former tourists about shooting gorillas were fibs or not. There were no English engineers, fresh from Great George Street, Westminster, writing home to the *Athenaeum* to say that they had just opened a branch railway up to Ephesus, and that (by the way) they had discovered a prae-Imperial temple of Juno the day before yesterday. Unprotected females didn't venture in "unwhisperables" into the depths of Norwegian forests; or, if they hazarded such undertakings their unprotectedness led them often to fall into cruel hands, and they never returned. A great fuss used to be made, before the days of steam, about the "Fair Sophia," who undertook a journey from Turkey to discover her lover, Lord Bateman; but how long and wearisome was her travail before she reached his lordship's castle in Northumberland, and was informed by the "proud young porter" that he was just then "taking of his young bride in"? Madame Cottin's Elizabeth, when she walked from Tobolsk to St. Petersburg to crave pardon for the exiles of Siberia; Sir Walter Scott's Jeanie Deans, when she tramped from Edinburgh to London on her errand of mercy, were justly regarded as heroines. But what were the achievements of those valorous young women when compared with the Ladies who make tours round Monte Rosa; nay, for the matter of that, "all round the world"? *Il n'y a plus de Pyrenees.* Nay, there are no more Andes, Himalayas, or Rocky Mountains. When the late Mr. Albert Smith wanted to change the attractions of his show, he calmly took a trip from Piccadilly to Hong Kong; it would have been better for him, poor dear fellow, had he remained at home. When her Majesty wanted to show the late Sultan of Turkey a slight act of civility, she sent Sir Charles Young out to Constantinople to invest Abdul Medjid with the Order of the Garter. Thirty years ago, it is possible the estimable King of Arms might have thought a mail-coach journey to York a somewhat serious expedition, yet he took the P. and O. Boat for Stamboul as blithely as though he were bound for a water-party at Greenwich. If an Emperor is to be crowned in Russia, or Prussia, or Crim Tartary, all the London newspapers despatch special correspondents to the scene of the pageant. Mr. Reuter will soon have completed his Overland Telegraph to China. At Liverpool they call New York "over the way." The Prince of Wales's travels in his nonage have made Telemachus a tortoise, and the young Anacharsis a stay-at-home. Married couples spend their honeymoon hippopotamus hunting in Abyssinia, or exploring the sources of the Nile. And the Traveller's Club are obliged to blackball nine-tenths of the candidates put up for election, because now-a-days almost every tolerably educated Englishman has travelled more than six hundred miles in a straight direction from the British Metropolis.

Bearing these facts in mind, the travels of Captain Dangerous, widely extended as they were, may not appear to the present generation as very uncommon or very surprising. But such travellers as my hero, formed, in the last century, a class apart, and were, in most cases, very strange men. Diplomatic agents belonging to the aristocracy rarely ventured beyond the confines of Europe. The Ambassadors sent to eastern climes were usually, although accredited from the English Court, maintained at the charge of great commercial corporations, such as the Turkey and Russia Companies, and were selected less on the score of their having handles to their names, or being born Russells, Greys, and Elliots, than because they had led roving and adventurous lives, and had fought in or traded with the countries where they were appointed to reside. Beyond these, the travelling class was made up of merchants, buccaneers, spies, and, notably, of political adventurers, and English, Scotch, and Irish Romanist Priests. The unhappy political dissensions which raged in this country from the time of the Great Rebellion to the accession of George the Third, and the infamous penal laws against the Roman Catholics, periodically drove into banishment vast numbers of loyal gentlemen and their families, and ecclesiastics of the ancient faith, who expatriated themselves for conscience' sake, or through dread of the bloody enactments levelled at those who worshipped God as their fathers had done before them. The Irish and Scotch soldiers who took service under continental sovereigns sprinkled the army lists of France, of Spain, and of Austria with O's and Macs. There was scarcely a European city without an Anglo-Saxon or Anglo-Celtic monastery or nunnery, and scarcely a seaport without a colony of British exiles cast upon foreign shores after the tempests of the Boyne, of Sheriffmuir, of Preston, or of Culloden. When these refugees went abroad it was to remain for ten, for twenty, for thirty years, or for life. The travelling of the present century is spasmodic, that of the last century was chronic.

I do not know whether the "Adventures" I have ascribed to Captain Dangerous will be readily recognised as "strange." To some they may appear exaggerated and distorted, to others merely strained and dull. If truth, however, be stranger than fiction, I may plead something in abatement; for although I am responsible for the thread of the story and the conduct of the narrative, there is not one Fact set down as having marked the career of the Captain that has been drawn from imagination. For the story of Arabella Greenville, for the sketch of the Unknown Lady, for the exploits of the "Blacks" in Charlwood Chase, for the history of Mother Drum, for the voyage round the world, for the details of the executions of Lord Lovat and Damiens, for the description of the state of a Christian captive among the Moors, I am indebted, not to a lively fancy, but to books of travel, memoirs, Acts of Parliament, and old newspapers and magazines. I can scarcely, however, hope that, although the incidents and the language in this book are the result of years of weary plodding and note-taking, through hundreds of dusty tomes, they will succeed in interesting or amusing the public now that they have undergone the process of condensation. The house need not be elegant because the foundations have been laboriously laid. A solid skeleton does not always imply a beautiful skin.

It is possible, nevertheless, that many persons may cry out that what I have written of Captain Dangerous could not have occurred, with any reasonable amount of probability, to any one man. Let me mention the names of a score of men and women recently or still living, and let me ask the reader whether anything in my hero's career was stranger than the adventures which marked theirs? Here is a penful taken at random,--Lord Dundonald, Lola Montes, Raousset-Boulbon, Richard Burton, Garibaldi, Felice Orsini, Ida Pfeiffer, Edgar Poe, Mr. and Mrs. Atkinson (the Siberian travellers), Marshal St. Arnaud, Paul du Chaillu, Joseph Wolff, Dr. Livingstone, Gordon Cumming, William Howard Russell, Robert Houdin, Constantine Simonides, Barnum, and Louis Napoleon Bonaparte. The life of any one of these personages, truthfully written, would be a thousand times stranger than anything that is set down to Dangerous's account. Let me quote one little example more in point. Two years ago I wrote a story called the "Seven Sons of Mammon," in which there was an ideal character--that of a fair-haired-little swindler, and presumable murderess, called Mrs. Armytage. The Press concurred in protesting that the character in question was untrue to nature, and, indeed, wholly impossible. Some details I had given of her violent conduct in prison were specially objected to as grossly improbable. I said at the time that I had drawn the woman from nature, and I was sneered at, and not believed. I now again declare, upon my honour, that this Mrs. Armytage, was a compound of two real people; that as regards her murdering propensities, I was, for the matter and the manner thereof, beholden to the French *Gazette des Tribunaux* for the year 1839; and that as respects her achievements in the way of lying, thieving, swindling, forging, and fascinating, I had before me, as a model, a woman whose misdeeds were partially exposed some ten years since in *Household Words*, who, her term of punishment over, is, to the best of my belief, alive at this moment, *and who was re-married less than a year ago*:--the announcement of that fact being duly inserted in the *Times* newspaper. The prison details had been gathered by me years before, in visits to gaols and in conversations with the governors thereof; and months after the publication of the "Seven Sons of Mammon," I found them corroborated in their minutest characteristics in a remarkable work called "Female Life in Prison."

   It remains for me to say one word as to the language in which the "Adventures of Captain Dangerous" are narrated. I had originally intended to call it a "Narrative in plain English;" but I found, as I proceeded, that the study of early eighteenth century literature--I mean the ante-Johnsonian period--had led me into the use of very many now obsolete words and phrases, which sounded like anything but plain English. Let me, however, humbly represent that the style, such as it is, was not adopted without a purpose, and that the English I have called "old-fashioned," was not in the remotest degree intended to be modelled upon the diction of Swift, or Pope, or Addison, or Steele, or Dryden, or Defoe, or even Nash or Howel. Such a feat of elegant pedantry has already been accomplished by Mr. Thackeray in his noble story of **Esmond**; and I had no wish to follow up a dignified imitation by a sorry caricature. I simply endeavoured to make Captain Dangerous express himself as a man of ordinary intelligence and capacity would do who was born in the reign of Queen Anne,--who received a scrambling education in that of George the First,-- who had passed the prime of his life abroad and had picked up a good many bastard foreign words and locutions,--whose reading had been confined to the ordinary newspapers and chap-books of his time (with perhaps an occasional dip into the pages of "Ned Ward" and "Tom Brown"),--and who in his old age had preserved the pseudo-didactic of his youth. The "Adventures of Captain Dangerous" have been, in every sense, an experiment, and not a very gratifying one. I have earned by them a great many kicks, but a very few halfpence. Should the toe of any friendly critic be quivering in his boot just now, at the bare announcement of "Captain Dangerous'" re-appearance, I would respectfully submit that there could not possibly occur a better opportunity than the present for kicking me **de novo**, as I have been for months very ill, and am weary, and broken.

GEORGE AUGUSTUS SALA.
BERNARD STREET, RUSSELL SQUARE,
April, 1863.

CHAPTER THE FIRST.

MINE OWN HOUSE.

I, JOHN DANGEROUS, a faithful subject of his Majesty King George, whose bread, God bless him! I have eaten, and whose battles I have fought, in my poor way, am now in my sixty-eighth year, and live in My Own House in Hanover Square. By virtue of several commissions, both English and foreign, I have a right to call myself Captain; and if any man say that I have no such right, he Lies, and deserves the Stab. It may be that this narrative, now composed only for my own Pleasure, will, long after my Death, see the light in Print, and that some copper Captain, or counterfeit critic, or pitiful creature of that kidney, will question my Rank, or otherwise despitefully use my Memory. Let such treachours and clapper-dudgeons (albeit I value not their leasing a bagadine) venture it at their peril. I have, alas, no heirs male; but to my Daughter's husband, and to his descendants, or, failing them, to their executors, administrators, and assigns, I solemnly commit the task of seeking out such envious Rogues, and of kicking and firking them on the basest part of their base bodies. The stab I forego; I wish not to cheat the hangman of his due, or the Rev. Mr. Villette of a sermon. But let the knaves discover, to the aching of their scald sides, that even the Ghost of John Dangerous is not to be libelled.

There is a knot of these same cittern-headed simpletons who meet at a coffee-house in Great Swallow Street, which I am sometimes minded to frequent, and who imagine that they show their wit and parts by reviling their Church and their King, and even by maligning the Honourable East India Company,--a corporation to which I am beholden for many Favours. "Fellow," I said, only last Saturday, to a whippersnapper from an Inn of Court,--a Thing I would not trust to defend my Tom-Cat were he in peril at the Old Bailey for birdslaughter, and who picks up a wretched livelihood, I am told, by scribbling lampoons against his betters in a weekly Review,--"Fellow," I said, "were I twenty years younger, and you twenty years older, John Dangerous would vouchsafe to pink an eyelet-hole in your waistcoat. Did I care to dabble in your polite conversation or your **belles lettres** (of which I knew much more than ever you will know years before the Parish was at pains to fix your begetting on some one), I would answer your scurrilities in Print; but this I disdain, sirrah. Good stout Ash and good strong Cordovan leather are the things fittest to meet your impertinences with;" and so I held out my Foot, and shook my Staff at the titivilitium coxcomb; and he was so civil to me during the rest of the evening as to allow me to pay his clog-shot for him.

The chief delight I derive from ending my days in Hanover Square is the knowledge that the house is Mine Own. I bought it with the fruit of mine own earnings, mine own moneys--not gotten from grinding the faces and squeezing the vitals of the Poor, but acquired by painful and skilful Industry, and increased by the lawful spoil of War. For booty, as I have heard a great commander say in Russia, is a Holy Thing. I have not disdained to gather moderate riches by the buying and selling of lawful Merchandize; albeit I always looked on mere Commerce and Barter as having something of the peddling and huxtering savour in them. My notion of a Merchant is that of a Bold Spirit who embarks on his own venture in his own ship, and is his own supercargo, and has good store of guns and Bold Spirits like himself on board, and sails to and fro on the High Seas whithersoever he pleases. As to the colour of the flag he is under, what matters it if it be of no colour at all, as old Robin Roughhead used to say to me,--even Black, which is the Negation of all colour? So I have traded in my way, and am the better by some thousands of pounds for my trading, now. That much of my wealth has its origin in lawful Plunder I scorn to deny. If you slay a Spanish Don in fair fight, and the Don wears jewelled rings and carcanets on all his fingers, and carries a great bag of muidores in his pocket, are you to leave him on the field, prithee, or gently ease him of his valuables? Can the crows eat his finery as well as his carcase? If I find a ship full of golden doubloons and silver candlesticks destined for the chapel of St. Jago de Compostella, am I to scuttle the ship and let her go down with all these good things on board; or am I to convey them to mine own lockers, giving to each of my Valiant Comrades his just and proper share? The governor of Carthagena will never get the doubloons, St.

Jago of Compostella will never see his candlesticks; why should not I and my Brave Hearts enjoy them instead of the fishes and the mermaids? They have Coral enough down there, I trow, by the deep, nini; what do they want with Candlesticks? If they lack further ornament, there are pearls enow to be had out of the oysters--unless there be lawyers down below--ay, and pearls, too, in dead men's skulls, and emerald and diamond gimmels on skeleton hands, among the sea-weed, sand, and the many-coloured pebbles of the great Ocean.

There are those who call me an old Pirate. Let them. I was never in trouble with the Admiralty Court. I can pass Execution Dock without turning pale. And no one can gainsay me when I aver that I have faithfully served his Majesty King George, and was always a true friend to the Protestant succession.

There has been a mighty talk, too, about my turning Turk. Why should not I, if I could not Help it? Better to read the Koran, than to sing the Black Sanctus. Better to serve Mahound than Bungy's dog. I never Turned my Tippet, as some fine gentlemen who have never seen Constantinople have done. I never changed my Principles, although I was a Bashaw with three tails. Better to have three tails than to be a Rat with only one. And, let me tell you, it is a mighty fine thing to be a Bashaw, and to have as many purses full of Sequins and Aspers as there are days in the year.

I should have been hanged long ago, should I--hanged for a Pirate, a Spy, and a Renegade? Well, I have escaped the bow-string in a country where hundreds die of Sore Throat every day, and I can afford to laugh at any prospect of a wych round my weasand in mine old age. Sword of Damocles, forsooth! why my life has been hanging on a cobweb any time these fifty years; and here I am at Sixty-Eight safe and sound, with a whole Liver and a stout Heart, and a bottle of wine to give a Friend, and a house of mine own in Hanover Square.

I write this in the great Front Parlour, which I have converted into a library, study, and counting-room. The year of our Lord is seventeen hundred and eighty. His Majesty's subjects have lost eleven days--through some Roguery in high places, you may be sure--since I was a young man; and were I a cocksloch, I might grudge that snipping off of the best part of a fortnight from an Old Man's life. It may be, indeed, that Providence, which has always been good to me, will add eleven days--yea, and twice eleven--to the dwindling span of poor old John Dangerous. I have many Mercies to be thankful for; of sins likewise without blin, and grievous ones, there may be a long list that I shall have to account for; but I can say that I never killed a man in cold blood, that I never wilfully wronged a woman, *so long as she was not obstinate*, that I never spake an unkind word to a child, that I always gave freely from that which I got freely, and never took from him who had little, and that I was always civil to the clergy. Yet Doctor Dubiety of St. George's tells me that I have been a signal sinner, and bids me, now, to repent of my evil ways. Dr. Dubiety is in the right no doubt;--how could a Doctor of Divinity be ever in the Wrong?--but I can't see that I am so much worse than other folks. I should be in better case, perhaps, if these eyes stood wider open. I confess that I have killed many men with Powder and Lead, and the sharp sword; but, then, had I not shot or stabbed them, they would surely have shot or stabbed me. And are not his Majesty's fellow-subjects shooting and stabbing one another at this instant moment[A] in the American plantations? No; I always fought fair, and never refused Quarter when mine enemy threw up his point; nor, unless a foeman's death were required for Lawful Reprisals, did I ever deny moderate Ransom.

There may be some things belonging to my worldly store that trouble me a little in the night season. Should I have given St. Jago de Compostella's candlesticks to Westminster Abbey? Why, surely, the Dean and Chapter are rich enough. But I declare that I had neither art not part in fitting the thumbscrews to the Spanish captain, and putting the boatswain and his mate to the ordeal of flogging and pickling. 'Twas not I, but Matcham, who is Dead, that caused the carpenter to be carbonadoed, and the Scotch purser to walk the Plank. Those were, I grant, deeds worthy of Blackbeard; but I had naught to do with them. John Dangerous had suffered too many tortures in the dungeons of the Inquisition to think of afflicting his fellow-creatures when there was no need for it. Then, as to what became of Dona Estella. I declare that I did my best to save that unhappy lady. I entreated, I protested; but in vain. None of that guilt lies at my door; and in the crime of him who roasted the Bishop, and cut off the Franciscan Monk's great-toes I have no share. Let every man answer for his own deeds. When I went the Middle Passage, I tried to keep the slaves alive as long I could. I was never a Mangoniser. When they died, what was there to do but to fling them overboard? Should I not have done the same by white men? I was not one of those cruel Guinea captains who kept the living and the dead chained together. I defy any one to prove it.

And all this bald chat about sacking towns and gutting convents? War is war all the world over; and if you take a town by Assault, why of course you must Sack it. As to gutting convents, 'tis a mercy to let some pure air into the close, stifling places; and, of a surety, an act of Charity to let the poor captive nuns out for a Holiday. Reverend Superiors, holy sisters, I never did ye any harm. You cannot torment me in the night. Your pale faces and shadowy forms have no need to gather round the bed of John Dangerous. Take, for Pity's sake, those Eyes away! But no more! These thoughts drive me Mad.

I am not Alone in my house. My daughter, my beloved Lilias, my only and most cherished child, the child of my old age, the legacy of the departed Saint her mother, lives with me. Bless her! she believes not a word of the Lies that are whispered of her old Father. If she were to be told a tithe of them, she would grieve sorely; but she holds no converse with Slanderers and those who wag their tongues and say so-and-so of such-a-one. She knows that my life has been wild, and stormy, and Dangerous as my name; but she knows that it has also been one of valour, and honesty, and striving. St. Jago de Compostella's candlesticks never went towards her schooling, pretty creature! My share from the gold in the scuttled ship never helped to furnish forth her dowry. Lilias is my joy, my comfort; my stay, my merciful consolation for the loss of that good and perfect Woman her mother. Dear heart! she has never been crossed in love, never known Love's sorrows, angers, disappointments, and despair. She was married to the Man of her Choice; and I am delighted to know that I never interfered, by word or by deed, with the progress of her Wooing; that he to whom she is wedded is one of the worthiest of youths; and that Heaven has blessed me with the means to enable him to maintain the state and figure of a gentleman.

Thus, although Comfort and Quiet are the things I chiefly desire after the bustle and turmoil of a tempest-tossed career, and the pleasure I take in the gaieties of the Town is but small, it cheers me to see my Son and Daughter enjoying themselves, as those who have youth and health and an unclouded conscience are warranted in doing, and, indeed, called upon to do. I like them on Sundays and Holidays to come to church at St. George's, and sit under Doctor Dubiety, where I, as a little lad, sat many and many a time, more than fifty years ago; but my house is no Conventicle, and on all weekdays and Lawful Occasions my family is privileged to partake to their heart's content of innocent and permitted pastimes. I never set my face against a visit to the Playhouse or to the Concert-room; although to me, who can remember the most famous players and singers of Europe, the King's Theatre and the Pantheon, and even Drury-Lane, are very tame places, filled with very foolish folk. But they please the young people, and that is enough for me. Nor to an occasional junketing at Vauxhall do I ever turn queasy. 'Tis true I have seen Ranelagh and Marylebone Belsize, and Spring Gardens, and seen Folly on the Thames--to say nothing of the chief Continental Tivolis, Spas, Lustgartens, and other places of resort of the Great; but fiddlers are fiddlers, and coloured lamps are coloured lamps, all the world over, I apprehend; and my children have as much delight in gazing on these spangled follies now as I had when I and the eighteenth century were young. Only against Masquerades and Faro-tables, as likewise against the pernicious game of E. O., post and pair, fayles, dust-point, do I sternly set my face, deeming them as wholly wicked, carnal, and unprofitable, and leading directly to perdition.

It rejoices me much that my son, or rather son-in-law,--but I love to call him by the more affectionate name,--is in no wise addicted to dicing, or horse-racing, or cock-fighting, or any of those sinful or riotous courses to which so many of our genteel youth--even to those of the first Quality--devote themselves. He is no Puritan; (for I did ever hate your sanctimonious Banbury-men); but he has a Proper Sense of what is due to the Honour and Figure of his family, and refrains from soiling his hands with bales of dice and worse implements among the profligate crew to be met with, not alone at Newmarket, or at the "Dog and Duck," or "Hockley Hole," but in Pall-Mall, and in the very ante-chambers of St. James's, no cater-cousin of the Groom-Porter he. He rides his hackney, as a gentleman should, nor have I prohibited him from occasionally taking my Lilias an airing in a neat curricle; but he is no Better on the Turf, no comrade of jockeys and stablemen, no patron of bruisers and those that handle the backsword and are quick at finish with the provant rapier, and agile in the use of the imbrocatto. I would disinherit him were I to suspect him of such practices, or of an over-fondness for the bottle, or of a passion for loose company. He hunts sometimes, and fishes and goes a birding, and he has a pretty fancy for the making of salmon-flies, in the which pursuit, I conclude, there is much ingenuity, and no manner of harm, fish being given to us for food, and the devising how best to snare the creatures entirely Lawful.

Lilias Dangerous has been wedded to Edward Marriner these two years. It was at first my design to buy the youth a Pair of Colours, and to let him see the world and the usages of honourable warfare for a year or two; but my Lilias could not bear the thought of her young Ensign's coming home without an arm or a leg, or perchance being slain in some desperate conflict with savage Indians, or scarcely less savage Americans; and I did not press my plan of giving Edward for a time to the service of the King. He, I am bound to say, was eager to take up a Commission; but the tears and entreaties of my Daughter, who thinks War the wickedest of crimes, and the shedding of human blood a wholly Unpardonable Thing, prevailed. So they were Married, and are Happy; and I am sure, now, that were I to lose either of them, it would break the old man's heart.

My Lilias is tall and slender, her skin is very white, her hair a rich brown, her eyes very large and clear and blue. But that I am too old to be vain, I might be twitted with Conceit when I state that she holds these advantages of person less from her Mother than from myself, her loving Father. Not that I was so comely in my young days; but my Grandmother before me was of the same fair Image that I so delight to look upon in Lilias. She was tall, and white, and brown-haired, and blue-eyed. She had Lilias's small and daintily-fashioned hands and feet, or rather Lilias has hers. To me these features were only transmitted in a meaner degree. I was a big-boned lusty lad, with flowing brown locks, an unfreckled skin, and an open eye; but my Grandmother's Face and Form have renewed themselves in my child. At twenty she is as beautiful as her Great-grandmother must have been at that same sunny time, as I am told and know that Lady was: albeit when I remember her she was nearly Ninety years of age.

Yes; Lilias's eyes are very blue; but they are always soft and tender and pitiful in their regard. Her Great-grandmother's had, when she was moved, a Strange Wild look that awed and terrified the beholders. Only once in the life of my Lilias, when she was very young, and on the question of some toy or sweetmeat which my departed Saint had denied her, did I notice that Terrible Look in her blue eyes. My wife, who, albeit the most merciful soul alive, ever maintained strict discipline in her household, would have corrected the child for what she set down as flat mutiny and rebellion; but I stayed her chastening hand, and bade the young girl walk awhile in the garden until her heat was abated; and as she went away, her little breast heaving, her little hands clenched, and the Terrible Look darting out on me through the silken tangles of her dear hair, I shuddered, and said, "Wife of mine, our Lilias's look is one she cannot help. It comes from Me, you may have seen it fiercer and fiercer in mine own eyes; and She, whom of all women I loved and venerated, looked thus when anger overcame her. And though I never knew my own dear Mother, she, or I greatly mistake, must have had that look in hers likewise."

I thank Heaven that those pure blue waters, limpid and bright, in my Lilias's orbs were nevermore ruffled by that storm. As she grew up, their expression became even softer and kinder, and she never ceased from being in the likeness of an Angel. She looks like one now, and will be one, I trust, some day, Above, where she can pray for her danger-worn old sire.

My own wife (whose name was Lilias too) was a merry, plump, ruddy-skinned little woman--a very baby in these strong arms of mine. She had laughing black eyes, and coal-black tresses, and lips which were always at vintage-time. Although her only child takes after me, not her, in face and carriage, in all things else she resembles my Saint. She is as merry, as light-hearted, as pure and good, as she was. She has the same humble, pious Faith; the same strong, inflexible will of abiding by Right; the same hearty, outspoken hatred of Wrong, abhorrence of Wrong. She has the same patience, cheerfulness, and obedience in her behaviour to those who are set in authority over her; and if I am by times angered, or peevish, or moody, she bears with my infirmities in the same meek, loving, and forgiving spirit. She has her Mother's grace, her Mother's voice, her Mother's ringing voice. She has her Mother's infinite care of and benevolence to the poor and needy. She has her Mother's love for merry sports and innocent romps. Like my departed Saint, she has an exquisitely neat and quick hand for making pastries and marchpanes, possets and sugared tankards, and confeeding of diapasms, pomanders, and other sweet essences, and cures for the chilblains; and like her she plays excellent well on the harpsichords.

Thus, in a quiet comfort and competence, in the love of my children, and in the King's peace, these my latter days are gliding away. I am somewhat troubled with gout and twitching pains, scotomies in the head, and fulness of humours, with other old men's ailments; and I do not sleep well o' nights owing to vexatious Dreams and

Visions, to abate which I am sometimes let blood, and sometimes blistered behind the ears; but beyond these cares--and who hath not his cares?--Captain John Dangerous, of number One hundred Hanover Square, is a Happy Man.

NOTE:
[A] 1780.

CHAPTER THE SECOND.

THE HISTORY OF AN UNKNOWN LADY, WHO CAME FROM DOVER
IN A COACH-AND-SIX.

IN the winter of the year 1720, died in her house in Hanover Square,--the very one in which I am now finishing my life,--an Unknown Lady nearly ninety years of age. The mansion was presumed to be her own, and it was as much hers as it is mine now; but the reputed landlord was one Doctor Vigors, a physician of the College in Warwick Lane, in whose name the Lease ran, who was duly rated to the poor as tenant, and whose patient the Unknown Lady was given out to be. But when Dr. Vigors came to Hanover Square it was not as a Master, but as the humblest of Servants; and no tradesman, constable, maid, or lacquey about the house or neighbourhood would have ventured for his or her life to question that, from cellar to roof, every inch of the mansion belonged to the Unknown Lady. The vulgar held her in a kind of Awe, and spoke of her as the Lady in Diamonds; for she always wore a number of those precious gems, in rings, bracelets, stomachers, and the like. The gentlefolks, of whom many waited upon her, from her first coming hither unto her death, asked for "my Lady," and nothing more. It was in the year 1714 that she first arrived in London, coming late at night from Dover, in a coach-and-six, and bringing with her one Mr. Cadwallader, a person of a spare habit and great gravity of countenance, as her steward; one Mistress Nancy Talmash, as her waiting-woman; and a Foreign Person of a dark and forbidding mien, who was said to be her chaplain. In the following year, and during the unhappy troubles in Scotland arising out of the treasons of the Earl of Mar, and other Scots Lords, one of his Majesty's messengers came for the Foreign Person, and conveyed him in a coach to the Cockpit at Whitehall; while another messenger took up his abode in the house at Hanover Square, lying in the second best bed-chamber, and having his table apart, for a whole week. From these circumstances, it was rumoured that the Unknown Lady was a Papist and Jacobite; that the seminary Priest, her confederate, was bound for Newgate, and would doubtless make an end of it at Tyburn; and that the Lady herself would be before many days clapt up in the Tower. But Signor Casagiotti, the Venetian Envoy, as a subject of the seignory, claimed the Foreign Person and obtained his release; and it was said that one of the great Lords of the Council came himself to Hanover Square to take the examination of the Unknown Lady, and was so well satisfied with the speech he had with her as to discharge her then and there from Custody,--if, indeed, she had ever been under any actual durance,--and promise her the King and Minister's countenance for the future. The Foreign Person was suffered to return, and thenceforward was addressed as Father Ruddlestone, as though he had some licence bearing him harmless from the penalties and praemunires which then weighed upon recusant persons. And I am given to understand that, on the evening of his enlargement, the same great Lord, being addressed in a jocular manner at the coffee-house by a Person of Honour, and asked if he had not caught the Pope, the Devil, and the Pretender in petticoats and diamonds, somewhere in St. George's parish, very gravely made answer, that some degrees of Loyalty were like Gold, which were all the better for being tried in the furnace, and that, although there had once been a King James, and there was now a King George, the lady, of whom perhaps that gentleman was minded to speak, had done a notable Thing before he was born, which entitled her to the eternal gratitude of Kings.

Although so old on her first coming to Hanover Square, and dwelling in it until her waiting-woman avowed that she was close on her Ninetieth year, the Unknown Lady preserved her faculties in a surprising manner, and till within a few days of her passing away went about her house, took the air from time to time in her coach, or in a chair, and received company. The very highest persons of Quality sought her, and appeared to take pleasure in her conversation. To Court, indeed, she never went; but she was visited more than once by an illustrious Prince; and many great nobles likewise waited upon her in their Birthday suits. On Birthnights there was Play in the great drawing-room, where nothing but gold was permitted to be staked.

Credible persons have described her to me as being, and supplemented mine own memory--in the extremest sunset of her life, when the very fray and pillings of her garment were come to, and no more stuff remained wherewith to piece it,--a person of Signal Beauty. She was of commanding stature, stooped very little, albeit she made use of a crutch-stick in walking, and had a carriage full of graciousness, yet of somewhat austere Dignity. No portion of her hair was visible under the thick folds of muslin and point of Alencon which covered her head, and were themselves half hidden by a hood of black Paduasoy; but in a glass-case in her cabinet, among other relics of which I may have presently to speak, she kept a quantity of the most beauteous chestnut tresses ever beheld. "These were my Love-Locks, child," I remember her saying to me once. I am ashamed to confess that, during my brief commerce with her, the dress she wore, which was commonly of black velvet, and the diamonds which glittered on her hands and arms and bosom impressed themselves far more forcibly on my memory than her face, which I have since been told was Beautiful. My informant bears witness that her eyes were Blue, and of an exceeding brightness, sometimes quite terrible to look upon, although tempered at most times by a Sweet Mildness; yet there were seasons when this brightness, as that of the Sun in a wholly cloudless sky, became Fierce, and burnt up him who beheld it. Time had been so long a husbandman of her fair demesne, had reaped so many crops of smiles and tears from that comely visage, that it were a baseness to infer that no traces of his husbandry appeared on her once smooth and silken flesh, for the adornment of which she had ever disdained the use of essences and unguents. Yet I am told that her wrinkles and creases, although manifold, were not harsh nor rugged; and that her face might be likened rather to a billet of love written on fair white vellum, that had been somewhat crumpled by the hand of him who hates Youth and Love, than to some musty old conveyance or mortgage-deed scrabbled on yellow, damp-stained, rat-gnawed parchment. Her hands and neck were to the last of an amazing Whiteness. The former, as were also her feet, very small and delicate. Her speech when moved was Quick, and she spoke as one accustomed to be obeyed; but at most seasons her bearing towards her domestics was infinitely kind and tender. Towards the Foreign Person, her Director, she always bore herself with edifying meekness. She was cheerful in company, full of ready wit, of great shrewdness, discretion, and observation; could discourse to admiration of foreign cities and persons of renown, even to Kings and Princes, whom she had seen and known; and was well qualified to speak on public affairs, although she seldom deigned to concern herself with the furious madness of Party. Mere idle prattle of Operas, and Play-books, and Auctions, and the like, was extremely distasteful to her; and although at that time a shameful looseness of manners and conversation obtained even among the Greatest persons in the land, she would never suffer any evil or immodest talk to be held in her presence; and those who wished to learn aught of the wickedness of the town and the scandals of High Life were fain to go elsewhere for their gossip.

I have said that her dress was to me the chief point of notice, and is that of which I retain the keenest remembrance. Her diamonds, indeed, had over me that strange fascination which serpents are said to have over birds; and I would sit with my little mouth all agape, and my eyes fixed and staring, until they grew dazed, and I was frightened at the solemn twinkling of those many gems. In my absurd child-way, it was to my fancy as though the Lady were some great Altar or Herse of State in a Church, and her Jewels so many Lamps kindled about her, and to be kept alive for ever. She robed habitually, as I have said, in Black Velvet; but on Birthnights, when more company than usual came, and there was play in the great drawing-room, she would wear a sack of sad-coloured satin; while, which was stranger still, on the thirtieth day of January in every year, at least so long as I can keep it in mind, she wore her sable dress; not her ordinary one, but a fuller garment, which had bows of Crimson Ribbon down the front and at the sleeves, and a great Crimson Scarf over the right shoulder, so as to come in saltire over her Heart. And on the day she made this change she wore no Diamonds, but Rubies in great number, and of great size. On that day, also, we kept an almost entire fast, and from morning to night I had nothing but a little cake and a glass of Red wine. From sunrise to sunset the Lady sat in her cabinet among her Relics; and I was bidden to sit over against her on a little stool. She would talk much, and, as it seemed to me wildly, in a language which I could not understand, going towards her relics and touching them in a strange manner. Then she would say to me, with a sternness that chilled the marrow in my bones, "Child, Remember the Day: Remember the Thirtieth of January." And she would often repeat that word, "Remember," rocking herself to and fro. And more than once she would say, "Blood for blood." Then Mistress Talmash would enter and assay to Soothe her, telling her that what was past was past, and could not be undone. Then she would take out a great Prayer-Book bound in Red leather, and which had this strange device raised in an embosture of gold, on either cover, and in a solemn voice read out long passages, which I afterwards learned were from that service holden on the anniversary of the martyrdom of King Charles the First. She would go on to read the Ritual for the King's Touching for the Evil, now expunged from our Liturgy; and then Mistress Talmash would pray her to read the joyful prayers for the twenty-ninth of May, the date of the happy restoration of King Charles the Second. But that she would seldom do, murmuring, "I dare not, I dare not. Tell not Father Ruddlestone." All these things were very strange to me; but I grew accustomed to them in time. And there seems to a solitary child, an immensity of time passing between his first beginning to remember and his coming to eight years of age.

There is one thing that I must mention before this Lady ceases to be Unknown to the reader. She was afflicted with a continual trembling of the entire Frame. She was no paralytic, for to the very end she could take her food and medicine without assistance; but she shook always like a very Aspen. It had to do with her nerves, I suppose; and it was perhaps for that cause she was attended for so many years by Doctor Vigors; but he never did her any good in that wise; and the whole College of Warwick Lane would, I doubt not, have failed signally had they attempted her cure. Often I asked Mistress Talmash why the Lady--for until her death I knew of no other name whereby to call her--shook so; but the waiting-woman would chide me, and say that if I asked questions she would shake me. So that I forebore.

Ours was a strange and solemn household. All was stately and well ordered, and--when company came--splendid; but the house always seemed to me much gloomier than the great Parish-Church, whither I was taken every Sunday morning on the shoulder of a tall footman, and shut up alone in a great Pew lined with scarlet baize, and where I felt very much like a little child that was lost in the midst of the Red Sea. Far over my head hung a gallery full of the children of Lady Viellcastel's charity-school; and these, both boys and girls, would make grimaces at me while the Psalms were being sung, until I felt more frightened than when I was on my little stool in the cabinet of relics, on the thirtieth of January. Just over the ledge of my pew I could see the clergyman, in his large white wig, leaning over the reading-desk, and talking at me, as I thought, in a mighty angry manner; and when he, or another divine, afterwards ascended the pulpit above, I used to fancy that it was only the same parson grown taller, and with a bigger wig, and that he seemed to lean forward, and be angrier with me than ever. The time of kneeling was always one of sore trouble to me, for I had to feel with my foot for the hassock, which seemed to lie as far beneath me as though it were, indeed, sunk at the bottom of the Red Sea. Getting up again was quite as difficult; and I don't think we ever attained the end of the Litany without my dropping my great red Prayer-Book--not the thirtieth-of-January one, but another affected to my especial use--with a Clang. On such occasions the pew-door would open, and the Beadle enter. He always picked up the book, and gave it me with a low bow; but he never omitted to tell me, in a deadly whisper, that if I had been one of Lady Viellcastel's boys, he'd skin me alive, he would.

The Unknown Lady did not attend the parish-church. She, and Mistress Talmash, and the Foreign Person, held a service apart. I was called "Little Master," and went with the footman. The fellow's name, I remember, was Jeremy. He used to talk to me, going and coming, as I sat, in my fine Laced Clothes, and my hat with a plume in it, and my little rapier with the silver hilt, perched on his broad shoulder. He used to tell me that he had been a soldier, and had fought under Colonel Kirk; and that he had a wife, who washed bands and ruffles for the gentlemen of the Life Guard, and drank strong waters till she found herself in the Roundhouse. Always on a Sunday morning, as the church-bells began to ring, the Unknown Lady would give me a Guinea to put into the plate after service. I remember that the year before she died, when I was big enough to walk with my hand in Jeremy's, instead of being carried, that he told me on Easter-Sunday morning that his wife was dead, and that he had two children in a cellar who had no bread to eat. He cried a good deal; and before we reached the church, took me into a strange room in a back-street, where there were a number of men and women shouting and quarrelling, and another, without his wig and with a great gash in his forehead, sprawling on the ground, and crying out "Lillibulero!" and two more playing cards on a pair of bellows. And they were all drinking from mugs and smoking tobacco. Here Jeremy had something to drink, too, from a mug. He put the vessel to my lips, and I tasted something Hot, which made me feel very faint and giddy. When we were in the open air again, he cried worse than ever. What could I do but give him my guinea? On our return, to

Hanover Square, the Lady asked me, according to her custom, what was the text, and whether I had put my money into the plate. She was not strict about the first; for I was generally, from my tenderness of years, unable to tell her more than that the gentleman in the wig seemed very angry with me, and the Pope, and the Prince of Darkness; but she alway taxed me smartly about the Guinea. This was before the time that I had learned to Lie; and so I told her how I had given the piece of gold to Jeremy, for that his wife was no more, and his children were in a cellar with nothing to eat. She stayed a while looking at me with those blue eyes, which had first their bright fierceness in them and then their kind and sweet tenderness. It was the first time that I marked her eyes more than her dress and her diamonds. She took me in her lap, and printed her lips--which were very soft, but cold--upon my forehead.

"Child," she said, "did I use thee as is the custom, thou shouldst be Whipped, not Kissed, for thy folly and disobedience. But you knew not what you did. Here are two guineas to put into the plate next Sunday; and let no rogues cozen you out of it. As for Jeremy," she continued, turning to Mistress Talmash, "see that the knave be stripped of his livery, and turned out of the house this moment, for robbing my Grandson, and taking him on a Sabbath morning to taverns, among grooms, and porters, and fraplers, and bullies."

Yes; the Unknown Lady was my Grandmother. I purpose now to relate to you her History, revealed to me many years after her death, in a manner to be mentioned at the proper time.

CHAPTER THE THIRD.

THE HISTORY OF MY GRANDMOTHER, WHO WAS A LADY OF CON-
SEQUENCE IN THE WEST COUNTRY.

MY Grandmother was born at Bristol, about the year 1630, and in the
reign of King Charles the First. She came of a family noted for their
long lives, and of whom there was, in good sooth, a proverb in the
West setting forth that "Bar Gallows, Glaive, and the Gout, every
Greenville would live to a hundred." Her maiden name was Greenville: she was
baptised Arabella; and she was the only daughter of Richard Greenville, an Esquire
of a fair estate between Bath and Bristol, where his ancestors had held their land
for three hundred years, on a Jocular Tenure of presenting the king, whenever he
came that way, with a goose-pie, the legs sticking through the crust. It was Esquire
Greenville's misfortune to come to his patrimony just as those unhappy troubles
were fomenting which a few years after embroiled these kingdoms in one great and
dismal Quarrel. It was hard for a gentleman of consequence in his own county, and
one whose forefathers had served the most considerable offices therein,--having
been of the Quorum ever since the reign of King Edward the Third,--to avoid mingling in some kind or another in the dissensions with which our beloved country
was then torn. Mr. Greenville was indeed a person of a tranquil and placable humour, to whom party janglings were thoroughly detestable; and although he leant
naturally, as beseemed his degree, towards the upholding of his Majesty's Crown
and Dignity, and the maintenance in proper Honour and Splendour of the Church,
he was too good a Christian and citizen not to shrink from seeing his native land
laid waste by the blind savageness of a Civil War. And although, he paid Cess and
Ship-money without murmuring, and, on being chosen a Knight of the Shire, did

zealously speak up in the Commons House of Parliament on the King's side (refusing nevertheless to make one of the lip-serving crowd of courtiers of Whitehall), and although, when churchwarden in his parish, he ever preserved the laudable custom of Whitsun and Martinmas ales for the good of the poor, and persisted in having the Book of Sports read from the pulpit,--he was averse from all high-handed measures of musketooning, and calivering, and gambriling those of the meaner sort, or those of better degree (as Mr. Hampden, Mr. Pym, and Another whom I shudder to mention), who, for Conscience' sake, opposed themselves to the King's Government. He was in this wise at issue with some of his hotter Cavalier neighbours, as, for instance, Sir Basil Fauconberg, who, whenever public matters were under question, began with "Neighbour, you must first show me Pym, Hampden, Haslerigge, and the rest, swinging as the Sign of the Rogue's Head, and then I will begin to chop Logic with you." For a long time Mr. Greenville, my Great-grandfather (and my enemies may see from this that I am of no Rascal Stock), cherished hopes that affairs might be brought to a shape without any shedding of Blood; but his hope proved a vain and deceiving one; ungovernable passions on either side caused not alone the drawing of the Sword, but the flinging away of the Scabbard; and my Grandmother was yet but a schoolmaid at Madam Ribotte's academy for gentlewomen at Bristol when that dreadful sinful war broke out which ended in the barbarous Murther of the Prince, and the Undoing of these kingdoms.

Mr. Greenville had two children: a son, whose name, like his own, was Richard, and who was born some five years before his sister Arabella. Even as a child this last named person was exceedingly beautiful, very gracious, fair, grave, and dignified of deportment, with abundant brown hair, and large and lustrous blue eyes, which, when the transient tempests of childhood passed over her, were ever remarked as having the wild, fierce look, shared in sometimes by the males of her family. Her mother, to her sorrow, died when she was quite a babe. The Esquire was passionately fond of this his only daughter; but although it was torture for him to part with her, and he retained her until she was thirteen years of age in his mansion-house, where she was instructed in reading and devotion, pickling and preserving (and the distilling of strong waters), sampler work, and such maidenly parts of education, by the housekeeper, and by a governante brought from London,--he had wisdom enough to discern and to admit that his daughter's genius was of a nature that required and demanded much higher culture than could be given to her in an old Country Seat, and in the midst of talk about dogs, and horses, and cattle, and gunning and ploughing, and the continual disputes of hot-headed Cavaliers or bitter Parliamentarians, who were trying who should best persuade my Great-grandfather to cast in his lot with one or the other of the contending parties. His son Richard had already made his election, and, it is feared, by taking up supplies on post obit from usurious money-scriveners in Bristol and London, had raised a troop of horse for the service of the King. Moreover, Arabella Greenville was of a very proud stomach and unbending humour. She might be Led, but would not be Driven. She adored her father, but laughed at the commands of the governante, and the counsels of the housekeeper, who knew not how either to lead or to rule her. It was thus determined to send her to Madam Ribotte's academy at Bristol,--for even so early as King Charles's time had outlandish and new-fangled names been found for Schools; and thither she was accordingly sent, with instructions that she was to learn all the polite arts and accomplishments proper to her station, that she was to be kept under a strict regimen, and corrected of her faults; but that she was not to be thwarted in her reasonable desires. She was to have her pony, with John coachman on the skewball sent to fetch her every Saturday and holiday; was not to be overweighted with tedious and dragging studies; and was by no means to be subject to those shameful chastisements of the Ferula and the Rod, which, even within my own time, I blush to say had not been banished from schools for young gentlewomen. To sum up, Miss Arabella Greenville went to school with a pocketful of gold pieces, and a play-chest full of sweet-cakes and preserved fruits, and with a virtual charter for learning as little as she chose, and doing pretty well as much as she liked.

Of course my Grandmother ran a fair chance of being wholly spoiled, and growing up to one of those termagant, mammythrept romps we used to laugh at in Mr. Colley Cibber's plays. The schoolmistress fawned upon her, for, although untitled, Esquire Greenville (from whom my descent is plain), and he was so much respected in the West, that the innkeepers were used to beseech him to set up achievements of his arms at the hotels where he baited on his journeys, was one of the most considerable of the County Gentry; the teachers were glad when she would treat them from her abundant store of play-money; and she was a kind of divinity among the schoolmaids her companions, to whom she gave so many cakes and sweetmeats that the apothecary had to be called in about once a week to cure many of surfeit. But this fair young flower-bed was saved from blight and choking weeds, first, by the innate rectitude and nobility of her disposition, which (save only when that dangerous look was in her eyes) taught her to keep a rein over her caprices, and subdue a too warm and vigorous imagination; next, by the entire absence of Vanity and Self-Conceit in her mind,--a happy state, which made her equally alive to her own faults and to the excellences of others; and, last, by her truly prodigious aptitude for polite learning. I have often been told that but for adverse circumstances Mrs. Greenville must have proved one of the most learned, as she was one of the wittiest and best-bred, women of her Age and Country. In the languages, in all manner of fine needlework, in singing and fingering instruments of music, in medicinal botany and the knowledge of diseases, in the making of the most cunning electuaries and syllabubs, and even in Arithmetic,--a science of which young gentlewomen were then almost wholly deficient,--she became, before she was sixteen years of age, a truly wonderful proficient. A Bristol bookseller spoke of printing her book of recipes (containing some excellent hints on cookery, physic, the casting of nativities, and farriery); and some excellent short hymns she wrote are, I believe, sung to this day in one of the Bristol free-schools. But the talent for which she was most shiningly remarkable was in that difficult and laborious art of Painting in Oils. Her early drawings, both in crayons and Chinese ink, were very noble; and there are in this House now some miniatures of her father, brother, and school-companions, limned by her in a most delicate and lovely fashion; but 'twas in oils and in portraiture of the size of life that she most surpassed. She speedily out-went all that the best masters of this craft in Bristol could teach her; and her pictures--especially one of her Father, in his buff coat and breastplate, as a Colonel of the Militia--were the wonder, not only of Bristol, but of all Somerset and the counties adjacent.

About this time those troubles in the West, with which the name of Prince Rupert is so sadly allied, grew to be of such force and fury as to decide Mr. Greenville on going to London, taking his daughter Arabella with him, to make interest with the Parliament, so that peril might be averted from his estate. For although his son was in arms for King Charles, and he himself was a gentleman of approved loyalty, he had done nothing of an overt kind to favour King or Parliament. He thus hoped, having ever been a peaceable and law-worthy gentleman, to preserve his lands from peril, and himself and family from prosecution; and it is a great error to suppose that many honest gentlemen did not so succeed in the very fiercest frenzy of the civil wars in keeping their houses over their heads, and their heads upon their shoulders. Witness worthy Mr. John Evelyn of Wotton and Sayes Court, and many other persons of repute.

While the Esquire was intent on his business at Westminster, and settling the terms of a Fine, without which it seemed even his peaceable behaviour could not be compounded, he lay at the house of a friend, Sir Fortunatus Geddings, a Turkey merchant, who had a fair house in the street leading directly to St. Paul's Church, just without Ludgate. The gate has been pulled down this many a day, and the place where he dwelt is now called Ludgate Hill. As he had much going to and fro, and was afraid that his daughter might come to hurt, both in the stoppage to her schooling, and in the unquietness of the times, he placed her for a while at a famous school at Hackney, under that notable governante Mrs. Desaguiliers. And here Mrs. Greenville had not been for many weeks ere the strangest adventure in the world-- as strange as any one of my own--befel her. The terrible battle of Naseby had by this time been fought, and the King's cause was wholly ruined. Among other Cavaliers fortunate enough to escape from that deadly fray, and who were in hiding from the vengeance of the usurping government, was the Lord Francis V----s, younger son to that hapless Duke of B----m who was slain at Portsmouth by Captain F----n. It seems almost like a scene in a comedy to tell; and, indeed, I am told that Tom D'Urfey did turn the only merry portion of it into a play; but it appears that, among other shifts to keep his disguise, the Lord Francis, who was highly skilled in all the accomplishments of the age, was fain to enter Mrs. Desaguiliers' school at Hackney in the habit of a dancing-master, and that as such he taught corantoes and rounds and qyres to the young gentlewomen. Whether the governante, who was herself a stanch royalist, winked at the deception, I know not; but her having done so is not improbable. Stranger to relate, the Lord Francis brought with him a Companion who was, forsooth, to teach French and the cittern, and who was no other than Captain Richard, son to the Esquire of the West country, and who was likewise inveterately pursued by the Usurper. The brother recognised his sister--to what joy and contentment on both their parts I need not say; but ere the false Dancing-Master had played his part many days, he fell madly in love with Arabella Greenville. To her sorrow and wretchedness, my poor Grandmother returned his Flame. Not that the Lord Francis stands convicted of any Base Designs upon her. I am afraid that he had been as wild and as reckless as most of the young nobles of his day; but for this young woman at least his love was pure and honourable. He made no secret of it to his fast friend, Captain Richard (my Grand-uncle), who would soon have crossed swords with the Spark had any villany been afloat; and he made no more ado, as was the duty of a Brother jealous of his sister's fair fame, but to write his father word of what had chanced. The Esquire was half terrified and half flattered by the honour done to his family by the Lord Francis. The poor young man was under the very sternest of proscriptions, and it was openly known that if the Parliament laid hold on him his death was certain. But, on the other hand, the Esquire loved his daughter above all things; and one short half-hour, passed with her alone at Hackney, persuaded him that he must either let Arabella's love-passion have its vent, or break her heart for ever. And, take my word for it, you foolish parents who would thwart your children in this the most sacred moment of their lives,--thwart them for no reasonable cause, but only to gratify your own pride of purse, avarice, evil tempers, or love of meddling,--you are but gathering up bunches of nettles wherewith to scourge your own shoulders, and strewing your own beds with shards and pebbles. Take the advice of old John Dangerous, who suffered his daughter to marry the man of her choice, and is happy in the thought that she enjoys happiness; and I should much wish to know if there be any Hatred in the world so dreadful as that curdled love, as that reverence decayed, as that obedience in ruins, you see in a proud haughty daughter married against her will to one she holds in loathing, and who points her finger, and says within herself, "My father and mother made me marry that man, and I am Miserable."

It was agreed amongst those who had most right to come to an agreement in the matter, that as a first step the Lord Francis V----s should betake himself to some other place of hiding, as more in keeping with Mrs. Greenville's honour; but that, with the consent of her father and brother, he should be solemnly betrothed to her; and that, so soon as the troubles were over, or that the price which was upon his head were taken off, he should become her husband. And there was even a saving clause added, that if the national disturbances unhappily continued, Mrs. Greenville should be privately conveyed abroad, and that the Lord Francis should marry her so soon after a certain lapse of time as he could conveniently get beyond sea. My Lord Duke of B----m had nothing to say against the match, loving his brother, as he did, very dearly; and so, in the very roughest of times, this truest of true loves seemed to bid fair to have a smooth course.

But alas the day! My Grandmother's passion for the young Lord was a very madness. On his part, he idolised her, calling her by names and writing her letters that are nonsensical enough in common life, but which are not held to be foolish pleas in Love's Chancery. When the boy and girl--for they were scarcely more--parted, she gave him one of her rich brown tresses; he gave her one of his own dainty love-locks. They broke a broad piece in halves between them; each hung the fragment by a ribbon next the heart. They swore eternal fidelity, devotion. Naught but Death should part them, they said. Foolish things to say and do, no doubt; but I look at my grizzled old head in the glass, and remember that I have said and done things quite as foolish forty--fifty years ago.

Nothing but Death was to part them; and nothing but Death so parted them. The Esquire Greenville, his business being brought to a pleasant termination, having paid his Fine and gotten his Safe-Conduct and his Redemption from Sequestration, betook himself once more to the West. His daughter went with him, nourishing her love and fondling it, and dwelling, syllable by syllable, on the letters which the Lord Francis sent her from time to time. He was in hopes, he said, to get away to Holland.

Then came that wicked business of the King's Murder. Mr. Greenville, as became a loyal gentleman, was utterly dismayed at that horrid crime; but to Arabella the news was as of the intelligence of the death of some loved and revered friend. She wept, she sobbed, she called on Heaven to shower down vengeance on the Murderers of her gracious Prince. She had not heard from her betrothed for many days, and those who loved and watched her had marked a strange wild way with her.

It was on the fourth of February that the dreadful news of the Whitehall tragedy came to her father's house. She was walking on the next day very moodily in the garden, when the figure of one booted and spurred, and with the stains of many days' travel on his dress, stood across her path. He was but a clown, a mere boor;

he had been a ploughboy on her father's lands, and had run away to join Captain Richard, who had made him a trumpeter in his troop. What he had to say was told in clumsy speech, in hasty broken accents, with sighs and stammerings and blubberings; but he told his tale too well.

The Lord Francis V----s and Captain Richard Greenville--Arabella's lover, Arabella's brother--were both Dead. On the eve of the fatal thirtieth of January they had been taken captives in a tilt-boat on the Thames, in which they were endeavouring to escape down the river. They had at once been tried by a court-martial of rebel officers; and on the thirtieth day of that black month, by express order sent from the Lord General Cromwell in London, these two gallant and unfortunate gentlemen had been shot to death by a file of musketeers in the courtyard of Hampton Court Palace. The trumpeter had by a marvel escaped, and lurked about Hampton till the dreadful deed was over. He had sought out the sergeant of the firing party, and questioned him as to the last moments of the condemned. The sergeant said that they died as Malignants, and without showing any sign of Penitence; but he could not gainsay that their bearing was soldier-like.

Arabella heard this tale without moving.

"Did the Captain--did my brother--say aught before they slew him?" she asked.

"Nowt but this, my lady: 'God forgive us all!'"

"And the Lord Francis, said he aught?"

"Ay; but I dunno loike to tell."

"Say on."

"'Twas t' Sergeant tould un. A' blessed the King, and woud hev' t' souldiers drink 's health, but they wouldno'. And a' wouldno' let un bandage uns eyes; an' jest befwoar t' red cwoats foired, a' touk a long lock o' leddy's hair from 's pocket and kissed un, and cried out 'Bloud for Bloud!' and then a' died all straight along."

Mrs. Arabella Greenville drew from her bosom a long wavy lock of silken hair,--his hair, poor boy!--and kissed it, and crying out "Blood for Blood!" she fell down in the garden-path in a dead faint.

She did not Die, however, being spared for many Purposes, some of them Terrible, until she was nearly ninety years of age. But her first state was worse than death; she lying for many days in a kind of trance or lethargy, and then waking up to raving madness. For the best part of that year, she was a perfect maniac, from whom nothing could be got but gibberings and plungings, and ceaseless cries of "Blood for Blood!" The heir-at-law to the estate, now that the Esquire's son was dead, watched her madness with a cautelous avaricious desire. He was a sour Parliament man, who had pinned his faith to the Commonwealth, and done many Awakening things against the Cavaliers, and he thought now that he should have his reward, and Inherit.

It was so destined, however, that my Grandmother should recover from that Malady. On her beauty it left surprisingly few traces. You could only tell the change that had taken place in her by the deathly paleness of her visage, by her never smiling, and by that Fierce Expression in her eyes being now an abiding instead of a passing one. Beyond these, she was herself again; and after a little while went to her domestic concerns, and chiefly to the cultivation of that pleasing art of Painting in Oils in which she had of old time given such fair promise of excellence. Her father would have had several most ingenious examples of History and Scripture pieces by the Italian and Flemish masters bought for her to study by,--such copies being then very plentiful, by reason of the dispersing of the collections of many noblemen and gentlemen on the King's side; but this she would not suffer, saying that it were waste of time and money, and, with astonishing zeal, applied herself to the branch of portraiture. From a little miniature portrait of her dead Lord, drawn by Mr. Cooper, she painted in large many fair and noble presentments, varying them according to her humour,--now showing the Lord Francis in his panoply as a man of war, now in a court habit, now in an embroidered night-gown and Turkish cap, now leaning on the shoulder of her brother, the Captain, deceased. And anon she would make a ghastly image of him lying all along in the courtyard at Hampton Court, with the purple bullet-marks on his white forehead, and a great crimson stain on his bosom, just below his bands. This was the one she most loved to look upon, although her father sorely pressed her to put it by, and not dwell on so uncivil a theme, the more so as, in Crimson Characters, on the background she had painted the words "Blood for Blood," But whatever she did was now taken little account of, for all thought her to be distraught.

By and by she fell to quite a new order in her painting. She seemed to take infinite pleasure in making portraitures of OLIVER CROMWELL, who had by this time become Lord Protector of the Commonwealth. She had never seen that Bold Bad Man (the splendour of whose mighty achievements must for ever remain tarnished by his blood-guiltiness in the matter of the King's Murther); but from descriptions of his person, for which she eagerly sought, and from bustos, pictures, and prints cut in brass, which she obtained from Bristol and elsewhere, she produced some surprising resemblances of him who was now the Greatest Man in England. She painted him at full and at half length--in full-face, profile, and three-quarter; but although she would show her work to her intimates, and ask eagerly "Is it like--is it like him?" she would never part with one copy (and there were good store of time-servers ready to buy the Protector's picture at that time), nor could any tell how she disposed of them.

This went on until the summer of the year 1657, when her father gently put it to her that she had worn the willow long enough, and would have had her ally herself with some gentleman of worth and parts in that part of the country. For the poor Esquire desired that she should be his heiress, and that a man-child should be born to the Greenville estate, and thus the heir-at-law, who was a wretched attorney at Bristol, and more bitter against kings than ever, should not inherit. She was not to be moved, however, towards marriage; saying softly that she was already wedded to her Frank in heaven,--for so she spoke of the Lord Francis V----s,--and that her union had been blessed by her brother Dick, who was in Heaven too, with King Charles and all the Blessed Army of Martyrs. And I have heard, indeed, that the unhappy business of the King's death was the means of so crazing, or casting into a Sad Celibacy and Devouring Melancholy, multitudes of comely young women who were born for love and delights, and to be the smiling mothers of many children.

So, seeing that he could do nothing with her, and loth to use any unhandsome pressure towards one whom he loved as the Apple of his Eye, the Esquire began to think it might divert her mind to more cheerful thoughts if she quitted for a season that part of the country (for it was at Home that she had received the dreadful news of her misfortune); and, Sir Fortunatus Geddings and his family being extremely willing to receive her, and do her honour, he despatched Arabella to London, under protection of Mr. Landrail, his steward, a neighbour of his, Sir Hardress Eustis, lending his Coach for the journey.

Being now come to London, every means which art could devise, or kindness could imagine, were made use of by Sir Fortunatus, his wife, and daughter, to make Arabella's life happier. But I should tell you a strange thing that came about at her father's house the day after she left it for the Town. Mr. Greenville chanced to go in a certain long building (by the side of his pleasure-pond) that was used as a boat-house, when, to his amazement, he sees, piled up against the wall, a number of pictures, some completed, some but half finished, but all representing the Lord Protector Cromwell. But the strangest thing about them was, that in every picture the canvas about the head was pricked through and through in scores of places with very fine clean holes, and, looking around in his marvel, he found an arbalist or cross-bow, with some very sharp bolts, and was so led to conjecture that some one had been setting these heads of the Protector up as a target, and shooting bolts at them. He was at first minded to send an express after his daughter to London to question her if she knew aught of the matter; but on second thoughts he desisted, remembering that in the Message, almost, (as the times stood) there was Treason, and concluding that, after all, it might be but some idle fancy of Arabella, and part of the Demi-Craze under which she laboured. For there could be no manner of doubt that the Pictures, if not the Holes in them, were of her handiwork.

Meanwhile Arabella was being entertained in the stateliest manner by Sir Fortunatus Geddings, who stood in great favour with the government, and had, during the troubles, assisted the Houses with large sums of money. There were then not many sports or amusements wherewith a sorrowing maiden could be diverted; for the temper of England's Rulers was against vain pastimes and junketings. The Maypoles had been pulled down; the players whipped and banished; the bear and bull baitings, and even the mere harmless minstrelsy and ballad-singing of the streets, all rigorously pulled down. But whatever the worthy Turkey merchant and his household could do in the way of carrying Arabella about to suppers, christenings, country gatherings, and so forth, was cheerfully and courteously done. Sir Fortunatus maintained a coach (for he was one of the richest merchants in the City of London), and in this conveyance Arabella was ofttimes taken to drive in Hyde Park, or towards the Uxbridge Road. 'Twas on one of these occasions that she first saw the Protector, who likewise was in his coach, drawn by eight Holstein mares, and attended by a troop of Horse, very gallantly appointed, with scarlet livery coats, bright gorgets and back-pieces, and red plumes in their hats.

"He is very like, very like," she murmured, looking long and earnestly at the grand cavalcade.

"Like unto Whom, my dear?" asked Mrs. Nancy Geddings, the youngest daughter of Sir Fortunatus, who was her companion in the coach that day.

"Very like unto him who is at Home in the West yonder," she made answer. "Now take me back to Ludgate, Nancy sweet, for I am Sick."

She was to be humoured in everything, and she was taken back as she desired. It chanced, a few days after this, that word came that his Highness the Lord Protector of the Commonwealth of England (for to such State had Oliver grown) designed to visit the City, to dine with the citizens at Guildhall. There was to be a great Pageant. He was to be met at Temple Bar by the Mayor and Aldermen, and to be escorted towards Cheapside by those city Trainbands which had done such execution on the Parliament side during the wars, and by the Companies with their Livery banners. Foreign Ambassadors were to bear him company; for Oliver was then at the height of his power, and had made the name of England dreaded, and even his own prowess respected, by all nations that were beyond sea. He was to hear a sermon at Bow Church at noon, and at two o'clock--for the preacher was to be Mr. Hugh Peters, who always gave his congregation a double turn of the hour-glass--he was to dine at the Guildhall, where I know not how many geese, bustards, capons, pheasants, ruffs and reeves, sirloins, shoulders of veal, pasties, sweet puddings, jellies, and custards, with good store of Rhenish and Buckrack and Canary, and Bordelais and Gascoin wines, were provided to furnish a banquet worthy of the day. For although the Protectorate was a stern sad period, and Oliver was (or had schooled himself to be) a temperate man, the citizens had not quite forgotten their love of good cheer; and the Protector himself was not averse from the keeping up some state and splendour, Whitehall being now well-nigh as splendid as in the late King's time, and his Highness sitting with his Make-Believe Lords around him (Lisle, Whitclocke, and the rest), and eating his meat to tuckets upon Trumpets, and being otherwise puffed up with Vanity.

The good folks with whom Arabella was sojourning thought it might help to cure her of her sad moping ways if she saw the grand pageant go by, and mingled in the merriment and feasting which the ladies of Sir Fortunatus's family--the Knight himself being bidden to the Guildhall--proposed to give their neighbours on the day when Oliver came into the City. To this intent, the windows of their house without Ludgate were all taken out of their frames, and the casements themselves hung with rich cloths and tapestries, and decked with banners. And an open house was kept, literally; meats and wines and sweets being set out in every room, even to the bed-chambers, and all of the Turkey merchant's acquaintance being bidden to come in and help themselves, and take a squeeze at the windows to see his Highness go by. Only one window on the first floor was set apart, and here sat the Ladies of the family, with Mistress Deborah Clay, the Remembrancer's lady, and one that was sister to a Judge of Commonwealth's Bench, and Arabella Greenville, who was, for a wonder, quite cheerful and sprightly that morning, and who had for her neighbour one Lady Lisle, the wife of John Lisle, one of Cromwell's Chief Councillors and Commissioners of the Great Seal.[B]

The time that passed between their taking seats and the coming of the pageant was passed pleasantly enough; not in drinking of healths, which practice was then considered as closely akin to an unlawful thing, but in laughing and quaffing, and whispering of merry jests. For I have usually found that, be the Rule of Church and State ever so sour and stern, folks *will* laugh and quaff and jest on the sly, and be merry in the green tree, if they are forced to be sad in the dry.

There was a gentleman standing behind Arabella, a Counsellor of Lincoln's Inn I think, who was telling a droll story of Lord President Bradshaw to his friend from the Temple. Not greatly a person of whom to relate merry tales, I should think, that terrible Bencher, who sat at the head of the High Commission, clothed in his scarlet robe, and passed judgment upon his lord the King. But still these gentlemen laughed loud and long, as one told the other how the President lay very sick, sick almost to death, at his country house; and how, he being one that was in the Commission of the Chancellorship, had taken them away with him, and would by no means surrender them, keeping them under his pillow, night and day; wherefore one of his brother commissioners was fain to seek him out, and press him hard to give up the seals, saying that the business of the nation was at a Standstill, for they could neither seal patents nor pardons. But all in vain, Bradshaw crying out in a voice that, though weak, was still terrible, that he would never give them up, but would carry them with him into the next world; whereat quoth the other commissioner, "By ----, My Lord President, they will certainly melt if you do." And at this tale the gentleman from Lincoln's Inn and he from the Temple both laughed so, that Arabella, who had been listening without eavesdropping, burst into a fit of laughter too; only my Lady Lisle (who had likewise heard the Story) regarded her with a very grim and dissatisfied countenance, and murmured that she thought a little trailing up before the Council, and committing to the Gate-house, would do some popinjays some good, and cure them of telling tales as treasonable as they were scurrilous.

But now came a great noise of trumpets and hautboys and drums, and the great pageant came streaming up towards Ludgate, a troop of Oliver's own Body-guard on iron-grey chargers clearing the way, which they did with scant respect for the lives and limbs of the crowd, and with very little scruple either in bruising the Train-bands with their horses' hoofs and the flat of their broadswords. As Arabella leant forward to see the show approach, something hard, and it would seem of metal, that she carried beneath her mantle, struck against the arm of my Lady Lisle, who, being a woman of somewhat quick temper, cried out,

"Methinks that you carry a pocket-flask with you, Mistress Greenville, instead of a vial of essences. That which you have must hold a pint at least."

"I do carry such a flask," answered Arabella, "and please God, there are those here to-day who shall drink of it even to the Dregs."

This speech was afterwards remembered against her as a proof of her Intent.

All, however, were speedily too busy with watching the Show go by to take much heed of any word passage between the two women. Now it was Mistress Deborah Clay pointing out the Remembrancer to her gossip; now the flaunting banners of the Companies, now the velvet robes of the Lords of the Council were looked upon; now a Great Cry arose that his Highness was coming.

He came in his coach drawn by the eight Holstein mares, one of his lords by his side, and his two chaplains, with a gentleman of the bed-chamber sitting over against. He wore a rich suit of brown velvet purfled with white satin, a bright gorget of silver,--men said that he wore mail beneath his clothes,--startups and gauntlets of yellow Spanish, a great baldric of cloth-of-gold, and in his hat a buckle of diamonds and a red feather. Yet, bravely as he was attired, those who knew him declared that they had never seen Oliver look so careworn and so miserable as he did that day.

By a kind of Fate, he turned his glance upwards as he passed the house of the Turkey merchant, and those Cruel Eyes met the fierce gaze of Arabella Greenville.

"Blood for Blood!" she cried out in a loud clear voice; and she drew a Pistol from the folds of her mantle, and fired downwards, and with good aim, at the Protector's head.

My Lady Lisle saw the deed done. "Jezebel!" she shrieked, striking the weapon from Arabella's hand.

Oliver escaped unharmed, but by an almost miracle. The bullet had struck him as it was aimed, directly in the centre of his forehead, he wearing his hat much slouched over his brow; but it had struck--not his skull, but the diamond buckle, and glancing off from that hard mass, sped out of the coach-window again, on what errand none could tell, for it was heard of no more. I have often wondered what became of all the bullets I have let fly.

The stoppage of the coach; the Protector half stunned; the chaplain paralysed with fear; the Trainbands in a frenzy--half of terror, half of strong drink--firing off their pieces hap-hazard at the windows, and shouting out that this was a plot of the Papists or the Malignants; the crowd surging, the Body-Guard galloping to and fro; the poor standard-bearers tripping themselves up with their own poles,--all this made a mad turmoil in the street without Ludgate. But the Protector had speedily found all his senses, and had whispered a word or two to a certain Sergeant in whom he placed great trust, and pointed his finger to a certain window. Then the Sergeant being gone away, orders were given for the pageant to move on; and through Ludgate, and by Paul's, and up Chepe, and to Bow Church, it moved accordingly. Mr. Hugh Peters preached for two hours as though nothing had happened. Being doubtless under instructions, he made not the slightest allusion to the late tragic Attempt; and at the banquet afterwards at the Guildhall, there were only a few trifling rumours that his Highness had been shot at by a mad woman from a window in Fleet Street; denial, however, being speedily given to this by persons in Authority, who declared that the disturbance without Ludgate had arisen simply from a drunken soldier of the Trainbands firing his musketoon into the air for Joy.

But the Sergeant, with some soldiers of the Protector's own, walked tranquilly into the house of Sir Fortunatus Geddings, and into the upper chamber, where the would-be Avenger of Blood was surrounded by a throng of men and women gazing upon her, half in horror, and half in admiration. The Sergeant beckoned to her, and she arose without a murmur, and went with him and the soldiers, two only being left as sentinels, to see that no one stirred from the house till orders came. By this time, from Ludgate to Blackfriars all was soldiers, the crowd being thrust away east and west; and, between a lane of pikemen, Arabella was brought into the street, hurried through the narrow lanes behind Apothecaries' Hall, and so through the alleys to Blackfriars Stairs, where a barge was in waiting, which bore her swiftly away to Whitehall.

"You have flown at High Game, mistress," was the only remark made to her by the Sergeant.

She was locked up for many hours in an inner chamber, the windows being closed, and a lamp set on the table. They bound her, but, mindful of her sex and youth, not in fetters, or even with ropes, contenting themselves with fastening her arms tightly behind her with the Sergeant's silken sash. For the Sergeant was of Cromwell's own guard, and was of great authority.

At about nine at night the Sergeant and two soldiers came for her, and so brought her, through many lobbies, to Cromwell's own closet, where she found him still with his hat and baldric on, sitting at a table covered with green velvet.

"What prompted thee to seek my Life?" he asked, without anger, but in a slow, cold, searching voice.

"Blood for Blood!" she answered, with undaunted mien.

"What evil have I done thee, that thou shouldst seek my blood?"

"What evil--what evil, Beelzebub?--all! Thou hast slain the King my Lord and master. Thou hast slain the Dear Brother who was my playmate, and my father's hope and pride. Thou hast slain the Sweet and Gallant Youth who was to have been my husband."

"Thou are that Arabella Greenville, then, the daughter of the wavering half-hearted Esquire of the West."

"I am the daughter of a Gentleman of Long Descent. I am Arabella Greenville, an English Maid of Somerset; and I cry for vengeance for the blood of Charles Stuart, for the blood of Richard Greenville, for the blood of FRANCIS VILLIERS. Blood for Blood!"

That terrible gleam of Madness leapt out of her blue eyes, and, all bound as she was, she rushed towards the Protector, as though in her fury she would have spurned him with her foot, or torn him with her teeth. The Sergeant for his part made as though he would have drawn his sword upon her; but Oliver laid his hand on the arm of his officer, and bade him forbear.

"Leave the maiden alone with me," he said calmly; "wait within call. She can do no harm." Then, when the soldiers had withdrawn, he walked to and fro in the room for many minutes, ever and anon turning his head and gazing fixedly on the prisoner, who stood erect, her head high, her hands, for all their bonds, clenched in defiance.

"Thou knowest," he said, "that thy Life is forfeit."

"I care not. The sooner the better. I ask but one Mercy: that you send me not to Tyburn, but to Hampton Court; there to be shot to death in the courtyard by a file of musketeers."

"Wherefore to Hampton?"

"Because it was there you murdered my Lover and my Brother."

"I remember," the Protector said, bowing his head. "They were rare Malignants, both. I remember; it was on the same thirtieth of January that Charles Stuart died the death. But shouldst thou not, too, bear in mind that Vengeance is not thine, but the Lord's?"

"Blood for Blood!"

"Thou art a maiden of a stern Resolve and a strong Will," said the Protector, musingly. "If thou art pardoned, wilt thou promise repentance and amendment?"

"Blood for Blood!"

"Poor distraught creature," this Once cruel man made answer, "I will have no blood of thine. I have had enough," he continued, with a dark look and a deep sigh; "I am weary; and Blood will have Blood. But that my life was in Mercy saved for the weal of these kingdoms, thou mightst have done with me, Arabella Greenville, according to thy desires."

He paused, as though for some expression of sorrow; but she was silent.

"Thou art hardened," he resumed; "it may be that there are things that ***cannot*** be forgiven."

"There are," she said, firmly.

"I spare thy life," the Lord Protector continued; "but, Arabella Greenville, thou must go into Captivity. Until I am Dead, we two cannot be at large together. But I will not doom thee to a solitary prison. Thou shalt have a companion in durance. Yes," he ended, speaking between his teeth, and more to himself than to her, "she shall join Him yonder in his lifelong prison. Blood for Blood; the Slayer and the Avenger shall be together."

She was taken back to her place of confinement, where meat and drink were placed before her, and a tiring-woman attended her with a change of garments. And at day-break the next morning she was taken away in a litter towards Colchester in Essex.[C]

NOTES:

[B] This Lady Lisle was a very virulent partisan woman, and, according to my Grandmother's showing, was so bitter against the Crown that, being taken, when a young woman, to witness the execution of King Charles, and seeing one who pressed to the scaffold after the blow to dip her kerchief in the Martyr's blood, she cried out "that she needed no such relic; but that she would willingly drink the Tyrant's blood." This is the same Alice Lisle who afterwards, in King James's time, suffered at Winchester for harbouring two of the Western Rebels.

[C] Those desirous of learning fuller particulars of my Grandmother's History, or anxious to satisfy themselves that I have not Lied, should consult a book called *The Travels of Edward Brown, Esquire*, that is now in the Great Library at Montague House. Mr. Brown is in most things curiously exact; but he errs in stating that Mrs. Greenville's name was Letitia,--it was Arabella.

CHAPTER THE FOURTH.

MY GRANDMOTHER DIES, AND I AM LEFT ALONE, WITHOUT SO MUCH AS A NAME.

I HAVE sat over against Death unnumbered times in the course of a long and perilous life, and he has appeared to me in almost every shape; but I shall never forget that Thirtieth of January in the year '20, when my Grandmother died. I have seen men all gashed and cloven about--a very mire of blood and wounds,--and heads lying about on the floor like ninepins, among the Turks, where a man's life is as cheap as the Halfpenny Hatch. I was with that famous Commander Baron Trenck[D] when his Pandours--of whom I was one--broke into Mutiny. He drew a pistol from his belt, and said, "I shall decimate you." And he began to count Ten, "one, two, three, four," and so on, till he came to the tenth man, whom he shot Dead. And then he took to counting again, until he was arrived at the second Tenth. That man's brains he also blew out. I was the tenth of the third batch, but I never blenched. Trenck happily held his hand before he came to Me. The Pandours cried out that they would submit, although I never spoke a word; he forgave us; and I had a flask of Tokay with him in his tent that very after-dinner. I have seen a man keel-hauled at sea, and brought up on the other side, his face all larded with barnacles like a Shrove-tide capon. Thrice I have stood beneath the yardarm with the rope round my neck (owing to a king's ship mistaking the character of my vessel).[E] I have seen men scourged till the muscles of their backs were laid bare as in a Theatre of Anatomy; I have watched women's limbs crackle and frizzle in the flames at an Act of Faith, with the King and Court--ay, and the court-ladies too--looking on. I stood by when that poor mad wretch Damiens was pulled to pieces by horses in the Greve. I have seen what the plague could do in the galleys at Marseilles. Death and I have been boon companions and bedfellows. He has danced a jig with me on a plank, and ridden bodkin, and gone snacks with me for a lump of horse-flesh in a beleaguered town; but no man can say that John Dangerous had aught but a bold face to show that Phantom who frights nursemaids and rich idle people so.

And yet, now, I can recall the cold shudder that passed through my young veins when my Grandmother died. Of all days, too, that the Thirtieth of January should have been ordered for her passing away! It was mid-winter, and the streets were white with Innocent Snow when she was taken ill. She had not been one of those trifling and trivanting gentlewomen that pull diseases on to their pates with drums and routs, and late hours, and hot rooms, and carding, and distilled waters. She had ever been of a most sober conversation and temperate habit; so that the prodigious age she reached became less of a wonder, and the tranquillity with which her spirit left this darksome house of clay seemed mercifully natural. They had noticed, so early as the autumn of '19, that she was decaying; yet had the roots of life stricken so strongly into earth as to defy that Woodman who pins his faith to shaking blasts at first, but when he finds that windfalls will not serve his turn, and that although leaves decay, and branches are swept away, and the very bark is stripped off, the tree dies not, takes heart of grace, and lays about him with his Axe. Then one blow with the sharp suffices. So for many months Death seemed to let her be, as though he sat down quietly by her side, nursing his bony chin, and saying, "She is very old and weak; yet a little, and she must surely be mine." Mistress Talmash appeared to me, in the fantastic imagination of a solitary childhood, to take such a part, and play it to the Very Death; and there were sidelong glances from her eyes, and pressures of her lips, and a thrusting forth of her hands when the cordial or the potion was to be given, that seemed to murmur, "Still does she Tarry, and still do I Wait." This gentlewoman was never hard or impatient with my Grandmother; but towards the closing scene, for all the outward deference she observed towards her, 'twas she who commanded, and the Unknown Lady who obeyed. Nor did I fail to mark that her bearing was towards me fuller of a kind of stern authority than she had of aforetime presumed to show, and that she seemed to be waiting for me too, that she might work her will upon me.

The ecclesiastic Father Ruddlestone was daily, and for many hours, closeted with my kinswoman and benefactress; and I often, when admitted to her presence after one of these parleys, found her much dejected, and in Tears. He had always maintained a ghostly sway over her, and was in these latter days stern with her almost to harshness. And although I have ever disdained eavesdropping and couching in covert places to hear the foregatherings of my betters (which some honourable persons in the world's reckoning scorn not to do), it was by Chance, and not by Design, that, playing one wintry day in the Withdrawing-room adjoining the closet where my Grandmother still sat among her relics, I heard high words--high, at least, as they affected one person, for the lady's rose not above a mild complaint; and Father Ruddlestone coming out, said in an angry tone:

"My uncle saved the King's life when he was in the Oak, and his soul when he was at Whitehall; and I will do his bidding by you now."

"The Lord's will be done, not mine," my Grandmother said meekly.

Then Father Ruddlestone passed into the Withdrawing-room, and seeing me on a footstool, playing it is true at the Battle of Hochstedt with some leaden soldiers, and two wooden puppets for the Duke and Prince Eugene, but still all agape at the strange words that had hit my sense, he catches me a buffet on the ear, bidding me mind my play, and not listen, else I should hear no good of myself, or of what an osier wand might haply do to me. And that a change was coming was manifest even in this rude speech; for my Grandmother, albeit of the wise King's mind on the proper ordering of children, and showing that she did not hate me when I needed chastening, would never suffer her Domestics, even to the highest, to lay a finger upon me.

It was after these things, and while I was crying out, more in anger than with the smart of the blow, that she called me into her closet and soothed me, giving me to eat of that much-prized sweetmeat she said was once such a favourite solace with Queen Mary of Modena, consort of the late King James, and which she only produced on rare occasions. And then she bewailed my hurt, but bade me not vex her Director, who was a man of much holiness, full, when we were contrite, of healing and quieting words; but then, of a sudden, nipping me pretty sharply by the arm, she said:

"Child, I charge thee that thou abandon that fair false race, and trust no man whose name is Stuart, and abide not by their fatal creed." In remembrance of which, although I am by descent a Cavalier, and bound by many bonds to the old Noble

House,--and surely there was never a Prince that carried about him more of the far-bearing blaze of Majesty than the Chevalier de St. G----, and bears it still, all broken as he is, in his Italian retreat,--I have ever upheld the illustrious House of Brunswick and the Protestant Succession as by Law Established. And as the barking of a dog do I contemn those scurril flouts and obloquies which have of old times tossed me upon tongues, and said of me that I should play fast and loose with Jacobites and Hanoverians, drinking the King over the Water on my knees at night, and going down to the Cock-pit to pour news of Jacobites and recusants and other suspected persons into the ears of Mr. Secretary in the morning. Treason is Death by the Law, and legal testimony is not to be gainsaid; but I abhor those Iscariot-minded wretches, with faces like those who Torture the Saints in old Hangings, who cry, aha! against the sanctuaries, and trot about to bear false witness.[F]

There were no more quarrels between my Grandmother and her Director. Thenceforth Father Ruddlestone ruled over her; and one proof of his supremacy was, that she forewent the use of that Common Prayer-Book of our Anglican Church which had been her constant companion. From which I conjecture that, after long wavering and temporizing, even to the length of having the Father in her household, she had at length returned to or adopted the ancient faith. But although the Substance of our Ritual was now denied her, she was permitted to retain its Shadow; and for hours would sit gazing upon the torn-off cover of the book, with its device of the crown and crossed axes, in sad memory of K. C. 1st.

A most mournful Christmas found her still growing whiter and weaker, and nearer her End. At this ordinarily joyful season of the year, it was her commendable custom to give great alms away to the poor,--among whom at all times she was a very Dorcas,--bestowing not only gifts of money to the clergy for division among the needy, but sending also a dole of a hundred shillings to the poor prisoners in the Marshalsea, as many to Ludgate, and the Gatehouse, and the Fleet,--surely prisons for debt were as plentiful as blackberries when I was young!--and giving away besides large store of bread, meat, and blankets at her own door in Hanover Square: a custom then pleasantly common among people of quality, but now--when your parish Overseer, forsooth, eats up the very marrow of the poor--fallen sadly into disuse. They are for ever striking Poor's Rates against householders, and will not take clipped money; whereas in my day Private Charity, and a King's Letter in aid from the pulpit now and then, were enough; and, for my part, I would sooner see a poor rogue soundly firked at the post, and then comforted with a bellyful of bread and cheese and beer by the constable, and so passed on to his belongings, than that he should be clapped up in a workhouse, to pick oakum and suck his paws like a bear, while Master Overseer gets tun-stomached over shoulder of veal and burnt brandy at vestry-dinners. For it is well-known, to the shame of Authority, that these things all come out of the Poor Rate.

Ere my Grandmother was brought so low, she would sit in state on almsgiving morning, which was the day after Christmas; and the more decent of her bedesmen and bedeswomen would be admitted to her presence to pay their duty, and drink her health in a cup of warm ale on the staircase. Also the little children from Lady Viellcastel's charity-school would be brought to her by their governante to have cakes and new groats given to them, and to sing one of those sweet tender Christmas hymns which surely fall upon a man's heart like sweet-scented balsam on a wound. And the beadle of St. George's would bring a great bowpot of such hues as Christmas would lend itself to, and have a bottle of wine and a bright broad guinea for his fee; while his Reverence the rector would attend with a suitable present,--such as a satin work-bag or a Good Book, the cover broidered by his daughters,--and, when he sat at meat, find a bank-bill under his platter, which was always of silver. And I warrant you his Reverence's eyes twinkled as much at the bill as at the plum-porridge, and that he feigned not to see Father Ruddlestone, if perchance he met that foreign person on the staircase, or in the store-office where Mistress Nancy Talmash kept many a toothsome cordial and heart-warming strong water.

This dismal Christmas none of these pleasant things were done. My Lady gave one Sum to her steward, Mr. Cadwallader, and bade him dispose of it according to his best judgment among the afflicted, bearing not their creed or politics or parish in mind, but their necessities. And I was bereft of a joyful day; for in ordinary she would be pleased that I should be her little almoner, and hand the purses with the groats in them to the poor almsfolk. What has become, I wonder, of those good old customs of giving away things at Christmas-tides? Where is the Lord Mayor's dole of beef-pies to the vagrant people that lurk in St. Martin's-le-Grand, that new Alsatia? Where is the Queen's gift of an hundred pounds to the distressed people who took up quarters in Somerset House? Where are the thousand guineas which the

Majesty of England was used to send every New-Year's morning to the High Bailiff of Westminster to be parted among the poor of the Liberty? Nothing seems to be given nowadays. 'Tis more caning than cakes that is gotten by the charity children; and Master Collector, the Jackanapes, is for ever knocking at my door for Poor's Rates.

In the middle of January my Grandmother was yet weaker. Straw was laid before her door, and daily prayers--for of course the Rector knew nothing about Father Ruddlestone--were put up for her at St. George's. And I think also she was not forgotten in the orisons of those who attended the chapel of the Venetian Envoy, and in that permitted to the use of the French Ambassador. Doctor Vigors was now daily in attendance, with many other learned physicians, who almost fought in the antechambers on the treatment to be observed towards this sick person. One was for cataplasms of bran and Venice turpentine, another for putting live pigeons to her feet, another for a portion of hot wine strained through gold-leaf and mingled with hellebore and chips of mandrake. Warwick Lane suggested mint-tea, and Pall Mall was all for bleeding. This Pall Mall physician was about the most passionate little man, with the biggest ruffles and the tallest gold-headed cane I ever saw. His name was Toobey.

"Blood, sir! there's nothing like blood!" he would cry to Doctor Vigors; and he cried out for "blood, sir," till you might fancy that he was a butcher or a herald-at-arms, or a housewife making black puddings.

Says Doctor Vigors in a Rage, "You are nothing but a barber-surgeon, brother, and learnt shaving on a sheep's head, and phlebotomy on a cow that had the falling fever."

"Mountebank and quacksalver!" answers my passionate gentleman, "you bought your diploma from one that forges seamen's certificates in Sopar Lane. Go to, metamorphosed and two-legged ass! Where is your worship's stage in the Stocks Market, with pills to purge the vapours, and powders to make my lady in love with her footman, and a lying proclamation on every post, and a black boy behind you to beat on the cymbals when you draw out teeth with the kitchen pliers."

"Rogue!" screams Dr. Toobey, "but for the worshipful house we are in, I would batoon you to a mummy."

"Mummy forsooth!" the other retorts; "Mummy with a murrain! Why, you dug up your grandmother, and pounded her up with conserve of myrrh, and called the stuff King Pharaoh, that was sovereign to cure the strangury."

"Better to do that," quoth Toobey, calming down into mere give and take--for he had, in truth, done some droll things in mummy medicaments,--"than to have been a Fleet parson, that was forced to sell ale and couple beggars for a living, and turned doctor when he had cured a bad leg for one that had lain too long in the bilboes."

This was too much for Doctor Vigors, who had once been in orders, and was still a Nonjuror, winked at, for his skill's sake, by Authority. He was for rushing on the Pall-Mall mummy-doctor and tousling of his wig, when Mistress Talmash came out of her lady's closet, and told them that she was fainting. This was the way that doctors disagreed when I was young, and I fancy that they don't agree much better now.

She lingered on, however, still resolutely refusing to take to her bed, and seeing me, if only for a moment, every day, for yet another fortnight. On the Twentieth of January, it was her humour to receive the visit of a certain great nobleman. Very many of the quality had daily waited upon her, or had sent their gentlemen to inquire after her; but for many weeks she had seen none but her own household. The nobleman I speak of had lately come down from the Bath, where he had been taking the waters; for he was full of years, and of Glory, and of infirmities. A message went to his grand house in Pall Mall, and he presently waited on my Grandmother. He was closeted with her for an hour, when the tap of my Grandmother's cane against the wainscot summoned Mistress Talmash, and she, doing her errand, brought me into the presence.

"My Lord," whispered my Grandmother, as she drew me towards her, and gave me a kiss that was almost of a whisper too, so feebly gentle was it,--"My Lord Duke, will you be pleased to lay your hand on the boy's head and give him your blessing, and it will make him Brave."

He smiled sadly at her fancy, but did as she entreated. He laid a hand that was all covered with jewelled rings, and that shook almost as much as my Grandmother's, on my locks, and prattled out to me something about being a good boy and not playing cards. He, too, was almost gone. He had a mighty wig, and velvet clothes all covered with gold-lace, a diamond star, and broad blue ribbon; but his poor swollen legs were swathed in flannel, and he was so feeble that he had to be helped down-stairs by two lacqueys. I too ran down-stairs unchecked, and saw him helped, tottering, into his chair, a company of the Foot-guards surrounding it; for he was much misliked by the mobile at that time, and few cried, God bless him! Indeed, as the company moved away, I heard a ragged fellow (who should have been laid by the heels for it) cry, "There goes Starvation Jack, that fed his soldiers on boiled bricks and baked mortar."

"He is a Whig now," said my Grandmother to me, when I rejoined her; "but he was of the bravest among men, and in the old days loved the true King dearly."

When this man was young and poor, the mobile used to call him "Handsome Jack." When he was rich and old and famous, he was "Starvation Jack" to them. And of such are the caprices of a vain, precipitate age. But I am glad I saw him, Whig and pinchpenny as he was. I am proud of having seen this Great Captain and Prince of the Holy Roman Empire. The King of Prussia, the Duke of Cumberland, my Lord George Sackville, Marshal Biron, Duke Richelieu, and many of the chiefest among the Turkish bashaws, have I known and conversed with; but I still feel that Man's trembling hand on my head; my blood is still fired, as at the sound of a trumpet, by the remembrance of his voice; I still rejoice at my fortune in having set eyes, if only for a moment, on John Churchill, Duke of Marlborough.

It was on the Twenty-ninth of January (o.s.) that our servants, who had declared to having heard the death-watch ticking for days, asserted that those ominous sounds grew faster and faster, resolving themselves at length into those five distinct taps, with a break between, which are foolishly held by the vulgar to spell out the word DEATH. And although the noise came probably from some harmless insect, or from a rat nibbling at the wainscot, that sound never meets my ear--and I have heard it on board ship many a time, and in gaol, and in my tent in the desert--without a lump of ice sliding down my back. As for Ghosts, John Dangerous has seen too many of them to be frightened.[G]

That night I slept none. It was always my lot in that huge house to be put, little fellow as I was, in the hugest of places. My bed was as spacious as a Turkish divan. Its yellow silken quilt, lined with eiderdown, and embroidered with crimson flowers, was like a great waving field of ripe corn with poppies in it. When I lay down, great weltering waves of Bed came and rolled over me; and my bolster alone was as big as the cook's hammock at sea, who has always double bedding, being swollen with other men's rations. This bed had posts tall and thick enough to have been Gerard the Giant's lancing-pole, that used to stand in the midst of the bakehouse in Basing Lane; and its curtains of yellow taffety hung in folds so thick that I always used to think birds nestled among them. That night I dreamt that the bed was changed into our great red pew at St. George's, only that it was hung with dark velvet instead of scarlet baize, and that the clergyman in the pulpit overhead, with a voice angrier than ever, was reading that service for the martyrdom of K. C. 1st, which I had heard so often. And then methought my dream changed, and two Great Giants with heading-axes came striding over the bed, so that I could feel their heavy feet on my breast; but their heads were lost in the black sky of the bed's canopy. Horror! they stooped down, and lo, they were headless, and from their sheared shoulders and their great hatchets dripped, dripped, for ever dripped, great gouts of something hot that came into my mouth and tasted salt! And I woke up with my hair all in a dabble with the nightdews, with my Grandmother's voice ringing in my ears, "Remember the Thirtieth of January!" Mercy on me! I had that dream again last night; and the Giants with their axes came striding over these old bones--then they changed to a headless Spaniard and a bleeding Nun; but the voice that cried, "Remember!" spake not in the English tongue, and was not my Grandmother's. And the hair of my flesh stood up, as Job's did.

In the morning, when the clouds of night broke up from the pale winter's sky, and went trooping away like so many funeral coach-horses to their stable, they told me that my Grandmother was Dead; that she had passed away when the first cock crew, softly sighing "Remember." It was a dreadful thing for me that I could not, for many hours, weep; and that for this lack of tears I was reproached for a hardened ingrate by those who were now to be my most cruel governors. But I could not cry. The grief within me baked my tears, and I could only stare all round at the great desert of woe and solitude that seemed to have suddenly grown up around me. That morning, for the first time, I was left to dress myself; and when I crept down to the parlour, I found no breakfast laid out for me--no silver tankard of new milk with a clove in it, no manchet of sweet diet bread, no egg on a trencher in a little heap of salt. I asked for my breakfast, and was told, for a young cub, that I might get it in the kitchen. It would have gone hard with me if, in my Grandmother's time, I had entered that place to her knowledge; but all things were changed to me now, and when I entered the kitchen, the cook, nay, the very scullion-wench, never moved for me. John Footman sat on the dresser drinking a mug of purl that one of the maids had made for him. The cook leered at me, while another saucy slut handed me a great lump of dry bread, and a black-jack with some dregs of the smallest beer at the bottom. What had I done to merit such uncivil treatment?

By and by comes Mr. Cadwallader with a sour face, and orders me to my chamber, and get a chapter out of Deuteronomy by heart by dinner-time, "Or you keep double fast for Martyrdom-day, my young master," he says, looking most evilly at me.

"Young master, indeed," Mrs. Nancy repeated; "young master and be saved to us. A parish brat rather. No man's child but his that to hit you must throw a stone over Bridewell Wall. Up to your chamber, little varlet, and learn thy chapter. There are to be no more counting of beads or mumblings over hallowed beans in this house. Up with you; times are changed."

Why should this woman have been my foe? She had been a cockering, fawning nurse to me not so many months ago. Months!--yesterday. Why should the steward, who was used to flatter and caress me, now frown and threaten like some harsh taskmaster of a Clink, where wantons are sent to be whipped and beat hemp. I slunk away scared and cowed, and tried to learn a chapter out of Deuteronomy; but the letters all danced up and down before my eyes, and the one word "Remember," in great scarlet characters, seemed stamped on every page.

It should have been told that between my seventh and my eighth year I had been sent, not only to church, but to school; but my grandmother deeming me too tender for the besom discipline of a schoolmaster,--from which even the Quality were not at that time spared,--I was put under the government of a discreet matron, who taught not only reading and writing, but also brocaded waistcoats for gentlemen, and was great caudle-maker at christenings. It was the merriest and gentlest school in the town. We were some twenty little boys and girls together, and all we did was to eat sweetmeats, and listen to our dame while she told us stories about Cock Robin, Jack the Giant-Killer, and the Golden Gardener. Now and then, to be sure, some roguish boy would put pepper in her snuff-box, or some saucy girl hide her spectacles; but she never laid hands on us, and called us her lambs, her sweethearts, and the like endearing expressions. She was the widow of an Irish colonel who suffered in the year '96, for his share in Sir John Fenwick's conspiracy; and I think she had been at one time a tiring-woman to my Grandmother, whom she held in the utmost awe and reverence. I often pass Mrs. Triplet's old school-house in what is now called Major Foubert's Passage, and recall the merry old days when I went to a schoolmistress who could teach her scholars nothing but to love her dearly. It was to my Grandmother, a kind but strict woman, to whom I owed what scant reading and writing ken I had at eight years of age.

Rudely and disdainfully treated as I now was, my governors thought it fit, for the world's sake, that I should be put into decent mourning; for my grandmother's death could not be kept from the Quality, and there was to be a grand funeral. She lay in State in her great bedchamber; tapers in silver sconces all around her, an Achievement of arms in a lozenge at her head, the walls all hung with fine black cloth edged with orris, and pieced with her escocheon, properly blazoned; and she herself, white and sharp as waxwork in her face and hands, arrayed in her black dress, with crimson ribbons and crimson scarf, and a locket of gold on her breast. They would not bury her with her rubies, but these, too, were laid upon her bier, which was of black velvet, and with a fair Holland sheet over all.

Not alone the chamber itself, but the anterooms and staircase were hung from cornice to skirting with black. The undertaker's men were ever in the house: they ate and drank whole mountains of beef and bread, whole seas of ale and punch (thus to qualify their voracity) in the servants' hall. They say my Grandmother's funeral cost a thousand pounds, which Cadwallader and Mrs. Talmash would really have grudged, but that it was the will of the executors, who were persons of condition, and more powerful than a steward and a waiting-woman. In her own testament my Grandmother said nothing about the ordering of her obsequies; but her executors took upon them to provide her with such rites as beseemed her degree. In those days the Quality were very rich in their deaths; and, for my part, I dissent from the starveling and nipcheese performances of modern funerals. It is most true that a hole in the sand, or a coral-reef, full fathom five, has been at many times my likeliest Grave; but I have left it nevertheless in my Will--which let those who come after me dispute if they dare--that I may be buried as a Gentleman of long descent, with all due Blacks, and Plumes, and Lights, and a supper for my friends, and mourning cloaks for six poor men.

Why the doctors should have remained in the house jangling and glozing in the very lobby of Death, and eating of cold meats and drinking of sweet wine in the parlour, after the breath was out of the body of their patient and patroness, it passes me to say; as well should a player tarry upon the Stage long after the epilogue has been spoken, the curtain lowered, and the lights all put out. Yet were Pall Mall and Warwick Lane faithful, not only unto the death, but beyond it, to Hanover Square. A coachful of these grave gentlemen were bidden to the burial, although it was probable that words would run so high among them as for wigs to be tossed out of the windows. And although it is but ill fighting and base fence to draw upon a foe in a coach, I think (so bitter are our Physicians against one another) that they would make but little ado in breaking their blades in halves and stabbing at one another crosswise as they sat, with their handkerchiefs for hilts.

It was on the eighth night after her demise, and at half-past nine of the clock, that my Grandmother was Buried. I was dressed early in the afternoon in a suit of black, full trimmed, falling bands of white cambric, edged, and a little mourning sword with a crape knot, and slings of black velvet. Then Mrs. Talmash knotted round my neck a mourning-cloak that was about eight-times too large for me, and with no gentle hand flattened on my head a hat bordered by heavy sable plumes. On the left shoulder of my cloak there was embroidered in gold and coloured silks a little escocheon of arms; and with this, in my child-like way, my fingers hankered to play; but with threats that to me were dreadful, and not without sundry nips and pinches, and sly clouts, I was bidden to be still, and stir not from a certain stool apportioned to me in the great Withdrawing-room. Not on this side of the tomb shall I forget the weary, dreary sense of desolation that came over me when, thus equipped, or rather swaddled and hampered in garments strange to me, and of which I scarcely knew the meaning, I was left alone for many hours in a dismal room, whose ancient splendour was now all under the eclipse wrought by the undertakers. And I pray that few children may so cruelly and suddenly have their happiness taken away from them, and from pampered darlings become all at once despised and friendless outcasts.

By and by the house began to fill with company; and one that was acting as Groom of the Chambers, and marshalling the guests to their places, I heard whisper to the Harbinger, who first called out the names at the Stair-head, that Clarencieux king-at-arms (who was then wont to attend the funerals of the Quality, and to be gratified with heavy fees for his office; although in our days 'tis only public noblemen, generals, ambassadors, and the like, who are so honoured at their interment, only undertaker's pageantry being permitted to the private sort)--that Clarencieux himself might have attended to marshal the following, and proclaim the Style of the Departed; but that it was ordered by authority that, as in her life her name and honours had been kept secret, so likewise in her death she was to remain an Unknown Lady. How such a reticence was found to jump with the dictates of the law, which required a registry of all dead persons in the parish-books, I know not; but in that time there were many things suffered to the Great which to the meaner kind would have been sternly denied; and, indeed, I have since heard tell that sufferance even went beyond the concealment of her Name, and that she was not even buried in woollen,--a thing then very strictly insisted upon, in order to encourage the staple manufactures of Lancashire and the North,--and that, either by a Faculty from the Arches Court, or a winking and conniving of Authority, she was placed in her coffin in the same garb in which she had lain in state. Of such sorry mocks and sneers as to the velvet of her funeral coffer being nearer Purple than Crimson in its hue, and of my mourning cloak being edged with a narrow strip of a Violet tinge,--as though to hint in some wise that my Grandmother was foregathered, either by descent or by marital alliance, with Royalty,--I take little account. 'Tis not every one who is sprung from the loins of a King who cares to publish the particulars of his lineage, and John Dangerous may perchance be one of such discreet men.

The doctors had been so long in the house that their names and their faces were familiar to me, not indeed as friends, but as that kind of acquaintance one may see every day for twenty years, and be not very grieved some morning if news comes that they are dead. Such an eye-acquaintance passes my windows every morning. I know his face, his form, his hat and coat, the very tie of his wig and the fashion of his shoe-buckle; but he is no more to me than I am haply to him, and there would be scant weeping, I opine, between us if either of us were to die. So I knew these doctors and regarded them little, wondering only why they ate and drank so much, and could so ill conceal their hatred as to be calling foul names, and well-nigh threatening fisticuffs, while the corpse of my Grandmother was in the house. But of the body of those who were bidden to this sad ceremony, I had no knowledge whatsoever. For aught I knew, they might have been players or bullies and Piccadilly captains, or mere undertaker's men dressed up in fine clothes; yet, believe me, it is no foolish pride, or a dead vanity, that prompts me to surmise that there were those who came to my Grandmother's funeral who had a Claim to be reckoned amongst the very noblest and proudest in the land. Beneath the great mourning cloaks and scarves, I could see diamond stars glistening, and the brave sheen of green and crimson ribbons. I desire in this particularity to confine myself strictly to the Truth, and therefore make no vain boast of a Blue Ribbon being seen there, thus denoting the presence of a Knight of the most noble Order of the Garter. I leave it to mine enemies to lie, and to cowardly Jacks to boast of their own exploits. This brave gathering was not void of women; but they were closely veiled and impenetrably shrouded in their mourning weeds, so that of their faces and their figures I am not qualified to speak; and if you would ask me that which I remember chiefly of the noble gentlemen who were present, I can say with conscience, that beyond their stars and ribbons, I was only stricken by their monstrous and portentous Periwigs, which towered in the candle-light like so many great tufts of plumage atop of the Pope's Baldaquin, which I have seen so many times staggering through the great aisles of St. Peter's at Rome.

Your humble servant, and truly humble and forlorn he was that night, was placed at the coffin's head; it being part of that black night's sport to hold me as chief mourner; and, indeed, poor wretch, I had much to mourn for. The great plumed hat they had put upon me flapped and swaled over my eyes so as almost to blind me. My foot was for ever catching in my great mourning cloak, and I on the verge of tripping myself up; and there was a hot smoke sweltering from the tapers, and a dreadful smell of new black cloth and sawdust and beeswax, that was like to have suffocated me. Infinite was the relief when two of the ladies attired in black, who had sat on either side of me, as though to guard me from running away, lifted me gently each under an armpit, and held me up so that I could see the writing on the coffin-plate, which was of embossed silver and very brave to view.

"Can you read it out, my little man?" a deep rich voice as of a lady sounded in mine ears.

I said, with much trembling, "that I thought I could spell out the words, if time and patience were accorded me."

"There is little need, child," the voice resumed. "I will read it to thee;" and a black-gloved hand came from beneath her robe, and she took my hand, and holding my forefinger not ungently made me trace the writing on the silver. But I declare that I can remember little of that Legend now, although I am impressed with the belief that my kinswoman's married name was not mentioned. That it was merely set forth that she was the Lady D----, whose maiden name was A. G., and that she died in London in the 90th year of her age, King George I. being king of England. And then the smoke of the tapers, the smell of the cloth and the wax, and the remembrance of my Desolation, were too much for me, and I broke out into a loud wail, and was so carried fainting from the room; being speedily, however, sufficiently recovered to take my place in the coach that was to bear us Eastward.

We rode in sorrowful solemnity till nigh three o'clock that morning; but where my Grandmother was buried I never knew. From some odd hints that I afterwards treasured up, it seems to me that the coaches parted company with the Hearse somewhere on the road to Harwich; but of this, as I have averred, I have no certain knowledge. In sheer fatigue I fell asleep, and woke in broad daylight in the great state-bed at Hanover Square.

NOTES:

[D] The Austrian, not the Prussian Trenck.--ED.

[E] This does not precisely tally with the Captain's disclaimer of feeling any apprehension when passing Execution Dock.--ED.

[F] I do not find it in the memoirs of his adventures, but in an old volume of the *Annual Register* I find that, in the year 1778, one Captain Dangerous gave important evidence for the crown against poor Mr. Tremenheere, who suffered at Tyburn, for fetching and carrying between the French King and some malcontents in this country, notably for giving information as to the condition of our dockyards.--ED.

[G] Captain Dangerous was, unconsciously, of the same mind with Samuel Taylor Coleridge.--ED.

CHAPTER THE FIFTH.

I AM BARBAROUSLY ABUSED BY THOSE WHO HAVE CHARGE OF
ME, AND FLYING INTO CHARLWOOD CHASE, JOIN THE "BLACKS."

IN the morning, the wicked people into whose power I was now delivered, came and dragged me from my bed with fierce thumps, and giving me coarse and rude apparel, forced me to dress myself like a beggar boy. I had a wretched little frock and breeches of grey frieze, ribbed woollen hose and clouted shoes, and a cap that was fitter for a chimney-sweep than a young gentleman of quality. I was to go away in the Wagon, they told me, forthwith to School; for my Grandmother--if I was indeed any body's Grandson--had left me nothing, not even a name. Henceforth, I was to be little Scrub, little Ragamuffin, little boy Jack. All the unknown Lady's property, they said, was left to Charities and to deserving Servants. There was not a penny for me, not even to pay for my schooling; but, in Christian mercy, Mrs. Talmash was about to have me taught some things suitable for my new degree, and in due time have me apprenticed to some rough Trade, in which I might haply--if I were not hanged, as she hinted pretty plainly, and more than once--earn an honest livelihood. Meanwhile I was to be taken away in the Wagon, as though I were a Malefactor going in a Cart to Tyburn.

I was taken down-stairs, arrayed in my new garments of poverty and disgrace, and drank in a last long look at my dear and old and splendid Home. How little did I think that I should ever come to look upon it again, and that it would be my own House--mine, a prosperous and honoured old man! The undertaker's men were busied in taking down the rich hangings, and guzzling and gorging, as was their wont, on what fragments remained of the banquetings and carousals of Death, which had lasted for eight whole days. All wretched as I was, I should--so easily are the griefs of childhood assuaged by cates and dainties--have been grateful for the wing of a chicken or a glass of Canary: but this was not to be. John a'Nokes or John a'Styles were now more considered than I was, and I was pushed and bandied about by fustian knaves and base mechanics, and made to wait for full half an hour in the hall, as though I had been the by-blow of a Running Footman promoted into carrying of a link.

'Twas Dick the Groom that took me to the Wagon. Many a time he had walked by the side of my little pony, trotting up the Oxford Road. He was a gross unlettered churl, but not unkind; and I think remembered with something like compunction the many pieces of silver he had had from his Little Master.

"It's mortal hard," he said, as he took my hand, and began lugging me along, "that your grandam should have died and left you nothing. 'Tis all clear as Bexley ale in a yard-glass. Lawyers ha' been reading the will to the gentlefolks, and there's nothing for thee, poor castaway."

I began to cry, not because my Grandmother had disinherited me, but because this common horse-lout called me a "castaway," and because I knew myself to be one.

"Don't fret," the groom continued; "there'll be greet enough for thee when thou'rt older; for thou'lt have a hard time on't, or my name's not Dick Snaffle."

We had a long way to reach the Wagon, which started from a Tavern called the "Pillars of Hercules," right on the other side of Hyde Park. I was desperately tired when we came thither, and craved leave to sit on a bench before the door, between the Sign-post and the Horse-trough. So low was I fallen. A beggar came alongside of me, and as I dozed tried to pick my pocket. There was nothing in it--not even a crust; and he hit me a savage blow over the mouth because I had nothing to be robbed of. Anon comes Dick Snaffle, who, telling me that the Saddler of Bawtry was hanged for leaving his liquor, and that he had no mind for a halter while good ale was to be drunk, had been comforting himself within the tavern; and he finding me all blubbered with grief at the blow I had gotten from the beggar, fetches him a sound kick; and so the two fell to fighting, till out comes the tapster, raving at Tom Ostler to duck the cutpurse cadger in the Horse-trough. There was much more sport out of doors in my young days than now.

At last the Wagon, for which we had another good hour to wait, came lumbering up to the Pillars of Hercules; and after the Wagoner had fought with a Grenadier, who wanted to go to Brentford for fourpence, and would have stabbed the man with his bayonet had not his hand been stayed, the Groom took me up, and put me on the straw inside. He paid the Wagoner some money for me, and also gave into his keeping a little bundle, containing, I suppose, some change of raiment for me, saying that more would be sent after me when needed; and so, handing him too a letter, he bade me Godd'en, and went on his way with the Grenadier, a Sweep, and a Gipsy woman, who was importunate that he should cross her hand with silver, in order that he might know all about the great Fortune that he was to wed, as Tom Philbrick did in the ballad. And this was the way in which the Servants of the Quality spent their forenoons when I was young.

As the great rumbling chariot creaked away westward, there came across my child-heart a kind of consciousness that I had been Wronged, and Cheated out of my inheritance. Why was I all clad in laces and velvet but yesterday, and to-day apparelled like a tramping pedlar's foster-brat? Why was I, who was used to ride in coaches, and on ponyback, and on the shoulder of my own body-servant, and was called "Little Master," and made much of, to be carted away in a vile dray like this? But what is a child of eight years old to do? and how is he to make head against those who are older and wickeder than he? I knew nothing about lawyers, or wills, or the Rogueries of domestics. I only knew that I had been foully and shamefully Abused since my dear Grandparent's death; and in that wagon, I think, as I lay tumbling and sobbing on that straw, were first planted in me those seeds of a Wild, and sometimes Savage, disposition that have not made my name to be called "Dangerous" in vain.

We were a small and not a very merry company under the wagon tilt. There was a Tinker, with all his accoutrements of pots and kettles about him, who was lazy, as most Tinkers are when not at hard work, and lay on his back chewing straw, and cursing me fiercely whenever I moved. There was a Welsh gentleman, very ragged and dirty, with a wife raggeder and dirtier than he. He was addressed as Captain, and was bound, he said, for Bristol, to raise soldiers for the King's Service. He beat his wife now and then, before we came to Hounslow. There was the tinker's dog, a great terror to me; for although he feigned to sleep, and to snore as much as a Dog can snore, he always kept one little red eye fixed upon me, and gave a growl and made a Snap whenever I turned on the straw. There was the Wagoner's child that was sickly, and continually cried for its mammy; and lastly there was a buxom servant-maid, with a little straw hat and cherry ribbons over a Luton lace mob, and a pretty flowered gown pulled through the placket-holes, and a quilted petticoat, and silver buckles in her shoes, and black mits, who was going home to see her Grandmother at Stoke Pogis,--so she told me, and made me bitterly remember that I had now no Grandmother,--and was as clean and bright and smiling as a new pin, or the milkmaids on May morning dancing round the brave Garlands that they have gotten from the silversmiths in Cranbourn Alley. She sat prettily crouched up on her box in a corner; and so, with the Tinker among his pots and kettles, the Welsh Captain and his lady on sundry bundles of rags, the sickly child in a basket, the Tinker's dog curled up in his Master's hat, I tossing on the straw, and a great rout of crates of crockery, rolls of cloth, tea and sugar, and other London merchandize, which the wagoner was taking down West, as a return cargo for the eggs, poultry, butcher's meat, and green stuff that he had brought up, made altogether such a higgledypiggledy that you do not often see in these days, when Servant-maids come up by Coach--my service to them!--and disdain the Wagon, and his Worship the Captain wears a fine laced coat and a cockade in his hat,--who but he!--and travels post.

The maid who was bound on a visit to her Grandmother was, I rejoice to admit, most tenderly kind to me. She combed my hair, and wiped away the tears that besmirched my face. When the Wagon halted at the King's Arms, Kensington, she tripped down and brought me a flagon of new milk with some peppermint in it; and she told me stories all the way to Hounslow, and bade me mind my book, and be a good child, and that Angels would love me. Likewise that she was being courted by a Pewterer in Panyer Alley, who had parted a bright sixpence with her--she showed me her token, drawn from her modest bodice, and who had passed his word to Wed, if he had to take to the Road for the price of the Ring--but that was only his funning, she said,--or if she were forced even to run away from her Mistress, and make a Fleet Match of it. It was little, in good sooth, that I knew about courtships or Love-tokens or Fleet Matches; but I believe that a woman, for want of a better gossip, would open her Love-budget to a Baby or a Blind Puppy, and I listened so well that she kissed me ere we parted, and gave me a pocketful of cheese-cakes.

It was quite night, and far beyond Hounslow, when I was dozing off into happy sleep again, that the Wagon came to a dead stop, and I awoke in great fright at the sound of a harsh voice asking if the Boy Jack was there. I was the "Boy Jack:" and the Wagoner, coming to the after-part of the tilt with his lantern, pulled me from among the straw with far less ado than if I had been the Tinker's dog.

I was set down on the ground before a tall man with a long face and an ugly little scratch wig, who had large boots with straps over his thighs like a Farmer, and swayed about him with a long whip.

"Oh, this is the boy, is it?" said the long man. "A rare lump to lick into shape, upon my word."

I was too frightened to say aught; but the Wagoner muttered something in the long man's ear, and gave him my bundle and money and the letter; and then I was clapped up on a pillion behind the long man, who had clomb up to the saddle of a vicious horse that went sideways; and he, bidding me hold on tight to his belt, for a mangy young whelp as I was, began jolting me to the dreadful place of Torture and Infernal cruelty which for six intolerable months was to be my home.

This man's name was Gnawbit, and he was my Schoolmaster. I was delivered over to him, bound hand and foot, as it were, by those hard-hearted folk (who should have been most tender to me, a desolate orphan) in Hanover Square. His name was Gnawbit, and he lived hard by West Drayton.

We are told in Good Books about the Devil and his Angels; but sure I think that the Devil must come to earth sometimes, and marry and have children: whence the Gnawbit race. I don't believe that the man had one Spark of Human Feeling in him. I don't believe that any tale of Man or Woman's Woe would ever have wrung one tear from that cold eye, or drawn a pang from that hard heart. I believe that he was a perfectly senseless, pitiless Brute and Beast, suffered, for some unknown purpose, to dwell here above, instead of being everlastingly kept down below, for the purpose of Tormenting. I was always a Dangerous, but I was never a Revengeful man. I have given mine enemy to eat when he was a-hungered, and to drink when he was athirst. I have returned Good for Evil very many times in this Troubled Life of mine, exposed as it has been always to the very sorest of temptations; but I honestly aver, that were I to meet this Tyrant of mine, now, on a solitary island, I would mash his Hands with a Club or with my Feet, if he strove to grub up roots; that were

I Alone with him, wrecked, in a shallop, and there were one Keg of Fresh Water between us, I would stave it, and let the Stream of Life waste itself in the gunwales while I held his head down into the Sea, and forced him to swallow the brine that should drive him Raving Mad. But this is unchristian, and I must go consult Doctor Dubiety.

Flesh and Blood! Have you never thought upon the Wrongs your Pedagogue has wrought upon you, and longed to meet that Wretch, and wheal his flesh with the same instrument with which he whealed you, and make the Ruffian howl for mercy? Mercy, quotha! did he ever show you any? A pretty equal match it was, surely! You a poor, weak starveling of a child shivering in your shoes, and ill-nurtured by the coarse food he gave you, and he a great, hulking, muscular villain, tall and long-limbed, and all-powerful in his wretched Empire; while you were so ignorant as not to know that the Law, were he discovered (but who was to denounce him?), might trounce him for his barbarity. Ah! brother Gnawbit, if I had ever caught you on board a good ship of mine! Aha! knave, if John Dangerous would not have dubbed himself the sheerest of asses, had he not made your back acquainted with nine good tails of three-strand cord, with triple knots in each, and the brine-tub afterwards. I will find out this Gnawbit yet, and cudgel him to the death. But, alas, I rave. He must have been full five-and-forty-years old when I first knew him, and that is nigh sixty years agone. And at a hundred and five the cruellest Tyrant is past cudgelling.

This man had one of the prettiest houses that was to be seen in the prettiest part of England. The place was all draped in ivy, and roses, and eglantine, with a blooming flower-garden in front, and a luscious orchard behind. He had a wife too who was Fair to see,--a mild little woman, with blue eyes, who used to sit in a corner of her parlour, and shudder as she heard the boys shrieking in the schoolroom. There was an old infirm Gentleman that lodged with them, that had been a Captain under the renowned Sir Cloudesley Shovel and Admiral Russell, and could even, so it was said, remember, as a sea-boy, the Dutch being in the Medway, in King Charles's time. This Old Gentleman seemed the only person that Gnawbit was afraid of. He never interfered to dissuade him from his brutalities, nay, seemed rather to encourage him therein, crying out as the sounds of torture reached him, "Bear it! bear it! Good again! Make 'em holloa! Make 'em dance! Cross the cuts! Dig it in! Rub in the brine! Oho! Bear it, brave boys; there's nothing like it!" Yet was there something jeering and sarcastic in his voice that made Gnawbit prefer to torture his unhappy scholars when the Old Gentleman was asleep,--and even then he would sometimes wake up and cry out, "Bear it!" from the attic, or when he was being wheeled about the neighbourhood in a sick man's chair.

The first morning I saw the Old Gentleman he shook his crutch at me, and cried, "Aha! another of 'em! Another morsel for Gnawbit. More meat for his market. Is he plump? is he tender? Will he bear it? Will he dance? Oho! King Solomon for ever." And then he burst into such a fit of wheezing laughter that Mrs. Gnawbit had to come and pat him on the back and bring him cordials; and my Master, looking very discomposed, sternly bade me betake myself to the schoolroom.

After that, the Old Gentleman never saw me without shaking his crutch and asking me if I liked it, if I could bear it, and if Gnawbit made my flesh quiver. Of a truth he did.

Why should I record the sickening experience of six months' daily suffering. That I was beaten every day was to be expected in an Age when blows and stripes were the only means thought of for instilling knowledge into the minds of youth. But I was alone, I was friendless, I was poor. My master received, I have reason to believe, but a slender Stipend with me, and he balanced accounts by using me with greater barbarity than he employed towards his better paying scholars. I had no Surname, I was only "Boy Jack;" and my schoolfellows put me down, I fancy, as some base-born child, and accordingly despised me. I had no pocket-money. I was not allowed to share in the school-games. I was bidden to stand aside when a cake was to be cut up. God help me! I was the most forlorn of little children. Mrs. Gnawbit was as kind to me as she dared be, but she never showed me the slightest favour without its bringing me (if her husband came to hear of it) an additionally cruel Punishment.

There was a Pond behind the orchard called Tibb's hole, because, as our schoolboy legend ran, a boy called Tibb had once cast himself thereinto, and was drowned, through dread of being tortured by this Monster. I grew to be very fond of standing alone by the bank of this Pond, and of looking at my pale face in its cool blue-black depth. It seemed to me that the Pond was my friend, and that within its bosom I should find rest.

I was musing in this manner by the bank one day when I felt myself touched on the shoulder. It was the crutch of the Old Gentleman, who had been wheeled hither, as was his custom, by one of the boys.

"You go into the orchard and steal a juicy pear," said the Old Gentleman to his attendant. "Gnawbit's out, and I won't tell him. Leave me with Boy Jack for five minutes, and then come back.--Boy Jack," he continued, when we were alone, "how do you like it?"

"Like what, sir?" I asked humbly.

"All of it, to be sure:--the birch, the cane, the thong, the ferula, the rope's-end,--all Gnawbit's little toys?"

I told him, weeping, that I was very, very unhappy, and that I would like to drown myself.

"That's wrong, that's wicked," observed the Old Gentleman with a chuckle; "you mustn't drown yourself, because then you'd lose your chance of being hanged. Gregory has as much right to live as other folks."[H]

I did not in the least understand what he meant, but went on sobbing.

"I tell you what it is," pursued the Old Gentleman; "you mustn't stop here, because Gnawbit will skin you alive if you do. He's bound to do it; he's sworn to do it. He half-skinned Tibb; and was going to take off the other half, when Tibb drowned himself like a fool in this hole here. He was a fool, and should have followed my advice and run away. 'Tibb,' I said, 'you'll be skinned. Bear it, but run away. Here's a guinea. Run!' He was afraid that Gnawbit would catch him; and where is he now? Skinned, and drowned into the bargain. Don't you be a Fool. You Run while there's some skin left. Gnawbit's sworn to have it all, if you don't. Here's a guinea, and run away as fast as ever your legs can carry you."

He gave me a bright piece of gold and waved me off, as though I were to run away that very moment. I submissively said that I would run away after school was over, but asked him where I should run to.

"I'm sure I don't know," the Old Gentleman said somewhat peevishly. "That's not my business. A boy that has got legs with skin on 'em, and doesn't know where to run to, is a jackass.--Stop!" he continued, as if a bright idea had just struck him; "did you ever hear of the Blacks?"

"No sir," I answered.

"Stupid oaf! Do you know where Charlwood Chase is?"

"Yes, sir; my schoolfellows have been nutting there, and I have heard them speak of it."

"Then you make the best of your way to Charlwood Chase, and go a-nutting there till you find the Blacks; you can't miss them; they're everywhere. Run, you little Imp. See! the time's up, and here comes the boy who stole the juicy pear." And the boy coming up, munching the remains of one of Gnawbit's juiciest pears, my patron was wheeled away, and I have never seen him from that day to this.

That very night I ran away from Gnawbit's, and made my way towards Charlwood Chase to join the "Blacks," although who those "Blacks" were, and whereabouts in the Chase they lived, and what they did when they were there, I had no more definite idea than who the Emperor Prester John or the Man in the Moon might be.

NOTE:

[H] In my youth ancient persons as frequently spoke of the hangman as "Gregory"--and he was so named at the trial of the Regicides in 1660-61--as by his later title of "Jack Ketch."--J. D.

CHAPTER THE SIXTH.

THE HISTORY OF MY GRANDFATHER, WHO WAS SO LONG KEPT
A PRISONER IN ONE OF THE KING'S CASTLES IN THE EAST COUN-
TRY.

AT the time when his Majesty Charles II. was so happily restored to the throne of these kingdoms, there was, and had been, confined for upwards of ten years, in one of his Majesty's Castles in the eastern part of this kingdom, a certain Prisoner. His Name was known to none, not even to the guards who kept watch over him, so to speak, night and day,--not even to the gaoler, who had been told that he must answer with his Head for his safe custody, who had him always in a spying, fretful overlooking, and who slept every night with the keys of the Captive's cell under his pillow. The Castle where he lay in hold has been long since levelled to the earth, if, indeed, it ever had any earth to rest upon, and was not rather stayed upon some jutting fragment of Rock washed away at last by the ever-encroaching sea. Nay, of its exact situation I am not qualified to tell. I never saw the place, and my knowledge of it is confined to a bald hearsay, albeit of the Deeds that were done within its walls I can affirm the certitude with Truth. From such shadowy accounts as I have collected, the edifice would seem to have consisted but of a single tower or donjon-keep very strong and thick, and defying the lashings of the waves, almost as though it were some Pharos or other guide to mariners. It was surrounded by a low stone wall of prodigious weight of masonry, and was approached from the mainland by a drawbridge and barbican. But for many months of the year there was no mainland within half a mile of it, and the King's Castle could only be reached by boats. Men said that the Sun never shone there but for ten minutes before and ten minutes after a storm, and there were almost always storms lowering over or departing from that dismal place. The Castle was at least two miles from any human habitation; for the few fishermen's cabins, made of rotten boats, hogsheads nailed together, and the like, which had pitifully nestled under the lee of the Castle in old time, had been rigorously demolished to their last crazy timber when the Prisoner was brought there. At a respectful distance only, far in, and yet but a damp little islet in the midst of the fens, was permitted to linger on, in despised obscurity, a poor swamp of some twenty houses that might, half in derision and half in civility, be called a Village. It had a church without a steeple, but with a poor Stump like the blunted wreck of some tall ship's mainmast. The priest's wages were less than those of a London coal-porter. The poor man could get no tithes, for there were no tithes to give him. Three parts of his glebe were always under water, and he was forced to keep a little school for his maintenance, of which the scholars could pay him but scant fees, seeing that it was always a chance whether their parents were dead of the Ague, or Drowned. Yet there was a tavern in the village, where these poor, shrinking, feverish creatures met and drank and smoked, and sang their songs, contriving now and again to smuggle a few kegs of spirits from Holland, and baffle the riding-officers in a scamper through the fens. They were a simple folk, fond of telling Ghost-Stories, and with a firm belief in charms to cure them from the Ague. And, with an awe whose intensity was renewed each time the tale was told, they whispered among themselves as to that Prisoner of Fate up at the Castle yonder. What this man's Crime had been, none could tell. His misdeed was not, it was whispered, stated in the King's Warrant. The Governor was simply told to receive a certain Prisoner, who would be delivered to him by a certain Officer, and that, at the peril of his life, he was to answer for his safe custody. The Governor, whose name was Ferdinando Glover, had been a Captain of Horse in the late Protector Oliver's time; but, to the surprise of all men, he was not dismissed at his Majesty's Restoration, but was continued in his command, and indeed, received preferment, having the grade of a Colonel on the Irish establishment. But they did not fail to tell him, and with fresh instances of severity, that he would answer with his head for the safe keeping of his Prisoner.

Of this strange Person it behoves me now to speak. In the year 1660, he appeared to be about seven-and-thirty years of age, tall, shapely, well-knit in his limbs, which captivity had rather tended to make full of flesh than to waste away; for there were no yards, nor spacious outlying walls to this Castle; and but for a narrow ledge that ran along the surrounding border, and where he was but rarely suffered to walk, there was no means for him to take any exercise whatever. He wore his own hair in full dark locks, which Time and Sorrow had alike agreed to grizzle. Strong lines marked his face, but age had not brought them there. His eye was dim, but more with watching and study than with the natural failing of vital forces.

So he had been in this grim place going on for twelve years, without a day's respite, without an hour's enlargement. True, he wore no fetters, and was treated with a grave and stately Consideration; but his bonds were not less galling, and the iron had not the less entered into his soul. The Order was, that he was to be held as a Gentleman, and to be subjected to no grovelling indignities or base usage. But the Order was (for a long time, and until another Prisoner, hereafter to be named, received a meed of Enlargement) likewise as strict that, save his keepers, he should see no living soul. "And it is useless," wrote a Great Lord to the Governor once, when it was humbly submitted to him that the Prisoner might need spiritual consolation, and have solace to his soul by conferring with poor Parson Webfoot yonder,--"it is useless," said that nobleman, "for your charge to see any black gown, under pretext that he would Repent; for, albeit though I know not his crime more than the babe unborn, I have it from his Majesty's own gracious word of mouth, that what he has done cannot be repented of; therefore you are again commanded to keep him close, and to let him have speech neither of parson nor of peasant." Which was duly done. But Colonel Glover, not untouched by that curiosity inherent to mankind, as well as womankind, took pains to cast about whether this was not one who had a hand in compassing the death of King Charles I.; and this coming, in some strange manner (through inquiries he had made in London), to the ears of Authority, he was distinctly told that his prisoner was not one of those bold bad men who, misled by Oliver Cromwell, had signed that fatal Warrant:--the names and doom of the Regicides being now all well known, as having suffered or fled from Justice, or being in hold, as Mr. Martyn was. So Colonel Glover, being well assured that what was done was for the King's honour, and for the well-being of his Estates, and that any other further searching or prying might cost him his place, if they did not draw him within the meshes of the law against Misprision of Treason, forbore to vex himself or Authority further on matters that concerned him not, and was so content to guard his Prisoner with greater care than ever. The Castle was garrisoned by but twelve men, and of these six were invalids and matrosses; but the other six were tall and sturdy veterans, who had been indeed of Oliver's Life-guard, and were now confirmed in their places, and with the pay, not of common soldiers, but of private gentlemen, by the King's own order. Their life was dreary enough, for they could hold but little comradeship with the invalids, whom they dubbed "grey-beards, drivellers, and kill-joys." But they had a guard-room to themselves, where they diced and drank, and told their ruffian stories, and sang their knavish catches, as is the manner, I suppose, for all soldiers to do in all countries, whether in camps or in cities. But their duty was withal of the severest. The invalids went snugly to bed at nine of the clock, or thereabouts, but the veritable men-of-war kept watch and ward all night, turn and turn about, and even when they slept took their repose on a bench, which was placed right across the Prisoner's door.

This much-enduring man--for surely no lot could be harder than his--to be thus, and in the very prime and vigour of manhood, cooped up in a worse than gaol, wherein for a long time he was even denied the company of captives as wretched as he,--this slave to some Mightier Will and Sterner Fate than, it would seem, mortal knowledge could wot of, bore his great Distress with an unvarying meekness and calm dignity. With him, indeed, they did as they listed, using him as one that was as Clay in the hands of the Potter; but, not to the extent of one tetchy word or fro-ward movement, did he ever show that he thought his imprisonment unjust, or the bearing of those who were set over him cruel. And this was not an abject stupor or dull indifference, such as I have marked in rogues confined for life in the Bagnios of the Levant, who knew that they must needs pull so many strokes and get so many stripes every day, and so gave up battling with the World, and grinned contumely at their gaolers or the visitors who came sometimes to point at them and fling them copper money. In the King's Prisoner there was a philosophic reserve and quiet-ness that almost approached content; and his resignation under suffering was of that kind that a Just Man may feel who knows that he is upon the ground, and that, howsoever his enemies push at him, he cannot fall far. He never sought to evade the conditions of his captivity or to plead for its being lightened. The courtesies that were offered to him, in so far as the Governor was warranted in offering such civili-ties, he took as his due; but he never craved a greater indulgence or went one step in word or in deed to obtain a surcease from his harsh and cruel lot.

He would rise at six of the clock both in winter and summer, and apply himself with great ardour to his private devotions and to good studies until eight, when his breakfast, a tankard of furmety and a small measure of wine, was brought him. And from nine until noon he would again be at his studies, and then have dinner of such meats as were in season. From one to three he was privileged to walk either on the narrow strip of masonry that encompassed his prison-house, and with a soldier with his firelock on hip following his every step, or else to wander up and down in the various chambers of the Castle, still followed by a guard. Now he would tarry awhile in the guard-room, and stand over against the soldier's table, his head resting very sadly against the chimney, and listen to their wild talk, which was, however, somewhat hushed and shaped to decency so long as he abided there. And anon he would come into the Governor's apartment, and hold Colonel Glover for some moments in grave discourse on matters of history, and the lives of Worthy Captains, and sometimes upon points and passages of Scripture, but never upon anything that concerned the present day. For, beyond the bounds of the place in which he was immured, what should he know of things of instant moment, or of the way the world was wagging? By permission, the Colonel had told him that Oliver was no more, and that Richard, his son, was made Protector in his stead. Then, at the close of that weak and vain shadow of a Reign, and after the politic act of my Lord Duke of Albemarle (Gen. Monk), who made his own and the country's fortune, and Nan Clarges'[I] to boot, at one stroke, the Prisoner was given to know that schism was at an end, and that the King had come to his own again. Colonel Glover must needs tell him; for he was bidden to fire a salvo from the five pieces of artillery he had mounted, three on his outer wall, and two at the top of his donjon-keep, to say nothing of hoisting the Royal Standard, which now streamed from the pole where erst had floated the rag that bore the arms of the Commonwealth of England.[J]

"I am glad," the Prisoner said, when they told him. "I hope this young man will make England happier than did his father before him." But this was after he was in hopes of getting some company in his solitude, and when he was cheerfuller.

It was about midway in his imprisonment when another Captive was brought to the King's Castle; but it was not until close upon the Restoration of King Charles II. that the two prisoners were permitted to come together. The second guest in this most dolorous place was a Woman, and that Woman was my Grandmother,

Arabella Greenville.

There is no use in disguising the fact that, for many months after the failure of her attack on the Protector, the poor Lady had been as entirely distraught as was her fate after the death of the Lord Francis, and that to write her Life during this period would be merely penning the chronicle of a continued Frenzy. It were merciful to draw a veil over so sad and mortifying a scene--so well brought up as she had been, and respected by all the Quality,--but in pursuit of the determination with which I set out, to tell the Truth, and all the Truth, I am forced to confess that my Grandmother's Ravings were of the most violent, and that of her thoroughly demented state there could be no doubt. So far, indeed, did the unhappy creature's Abandonment extend, that those who were about her could with difficulty persuade her to keep any Garments upon her body, and were forced with Stripes and Revilings to force to a decorous carriage the gentle Lady who had once been the very soul and mirror of Modesty. But in process of time these dreadful furies and rages left her, and she became calm. She was still beautiful, albeit her comeliness was now of a chastened and saddened order, and, save her eye, there was no light or sparkle in her face.

When her health and mind were healed, so far as earthly skill could heal them,--it being given out, I am told, to her kindred that she had died mad in the Spinning House at Cambridge: but she had never been further than the house of one Dr Empson at Colchester, who had tended her during her distraction,--my Grandmother was brought to the King's Castle in the East, and for a long time lay incarcerate in a lower chamber of the Keep, being not allowed even that scant exercise which was permitted to the Prisoner above, and being waited upon and watched night and day by the Governor's Daughter, Mistress Ruth Glover, who at nights slept in a little closet adjoining my Grandmother's chamber. The girl had a tongue, I suppose, like the rest of her sex,--and of our sex too, brother,--and she would not have been eighteen, of a lively Disposition, and continually in the society of a Lady of Birth and accomplishments, not more than ten years her senior, without gossiping to her concerning all that she knew of the sorry little world round about her. It was not, however, much, or of any great moment, that Ruth had to tell my Grandmother. She could but hold her in discourse of how the Invalid Matrosses had the rheumatism and the ague; how the Life-guard men in their room diced and drank and quarrelled, both over their dice and their drink; how the rumour ran that the poverty-stricken habitants of the adjoining village had, from long dwelling among the fens, become as web-footed as the wild-fowl they hunted; and how her Father, who had been for many years a widower, was harsh and stern with her, and would not suffer her to read the romances and play-books, some half-dozen of which the Sergeant of the Guard had with him. She may have had a little also to say about the Prisoner in the upper story of the Keep--how his chamber was all filled with folios and papers; how he studied and wrote and prayed; and during his two hours' daily liberty wandered sadly and in a silent manner about the Castle. For this was all Mistress Ruth had to tell, and of the Prisoner's name, or of his Crime, she was, perforce, mum.

These two Women nevertheless shaped all kinds of feverish Romances and wild conjectures respecting this unknown man above stairs. Arabella had told her own sad story to the girl who--though little better than a waiting-woman--she had made, for want of a better bower-maiden, her Confidante. I need not say that oceans of Sympathy, or the accepted Tokens thereof, I mean Tears, ran out from the eyes of the Governor's Daughter when she heard the History of the Lord Francis, of the words he spoke just before the musketeers fired their pieces at him, and of another noble speech he made two hours before he Suffered, when the Officer in command, compassionating his youth and parts, told him that if he had any suit, short of life, to prefer to the Lord General, he would take upon himself to say that it should be granted without question; whereon quoth my Lord Francis, "I will not die with any suit in my mouth, save to the King of kings." On this, and on the story of the Locket, and of his first becoming acquainted with Arabella, of his sprightly disguise as a Teacher, with the young squire at Madam Desaguilier's school at Hackney, of his Beauty and Virtues and fine manners and extraordinary proficiency in Arts and Letters and the Exercises of Chivalry,--of these and a thousand kindred things the two women were never tired of talking. And, indeed, if one calls to mind what vast Eloquence and wealth of words two loving hearts can distil from a Bit of Ribbon or a Torn Letter, it is not to be wondered at that Arabella and Ruth should find their Theme inexhaustible--so good and brave as had been its Object, now dead and cold in the bloody trench at Hampton yonder, and convert it into a perpetually welling spring of Mournful Remembrances.

Arabella had taken to her old trick of Painting again, and in the first and second year of her removal to the Castle executed some very creditable performances. But she never attempted either the effigies of her Lover or of the Protector, and confined herself to portraitures of the late martyred King, and of the Princes now unjustly kept from their inheritance.

It was during the Protectorate of Richard Cromwell (that mere puppet-play of Power) that the watch kept on the prisoners in the King's Castle grew for a time much less severe and even lax. Arabella was suffered to go out of her chamber, even at the very hours that the Prisoner above was wandering to and fro. The guards did not hinder their meeting; and, says Colonel Ferdinando Glover, one day to his daughter, "I should not wonder if, some of these days, Orders were to come down for me to set both my birds free from their cage. That which Mrs. Greenville has done, you and I know full well, and I am almost sorry that she did not succeed."

"Oh, father!" cries Mistress Ruth, who was of a very soft and tender nature, and abhorred the very idea of bloodshed; so that, loving Arabella as she did with all her heart, she could not help regarding her with a kind of Terror when she remembered the deed for which she was confined.

"Tush, girl," the Colonel makes answer, "'tis no Treason now to name such a thing. Oliver's dead, and will eat no more bread; and I misliked him much at the end, for it is certain that he betrayed the Good Old Cause, and hankered after an earthly crown. As for this young Popinjay, he will have more need to protect himself than these Kingdoms. And I think that if your father is to live on the King's wages, it had better be on the real King's than the false one."

"And do you think, father, that King Charles will come to his own again?" asks Ruth, in a flutter of delight; for Arabella had made her a very Royalist at heart.

"I think what I think," replies the Colonel, with his stern look; "but whatever happens, it is not likely, it seems me, that we shall have our prisoners here much longer. That is to say:--Mrs. Greenville, for what she hath done can scarcely be distasteful to those who loved not Oliver. But for my other bird,--who can tell? He may have raised the very Devil for aught I know."

"Do you think that he also tried to kill the Protector?" Ruth asks timidly, and just hazarding a Surmise that had oft been mooted betwixt Arabella and herself.

"Get thee to thy chamber, and about thy business, wench," the Colonel says, quite storming. "Away, or I will lay my willow wand about thy shoulders. Is there nothing but killing of Protectors, forsooth, for thy silly head to be filled with?" And yet I incline to think that Mr. Governor was not of a very different mind to his daughter; for away he hies to his chamber, and falls to reading Colonel Titus' famous book, ***Killing no Murder***, and, looking anon on his Prisoner coming wandering down a winding staircase, says softly to himself, "He looks like one, for all his studious guise, who could do a Bold Deed at a pinch."

This Person, I should have said, wore, winter and summer, a plain black shag gown untrimmed, with camlet netherstocks, and a smooth band. And his Right Hand was always covered with a glove of Black Velvet.

By and by came, as I have related, the news of his Majesty's Restoration and fresh Strict Orders for the keeping of the Prisoner. But though he was not to see a clergyman,--and for all that prohibition he saw more than one before he came out of Captivity,--a certain Indulgence was now granted him. He was permitted to have free access to Mrs. Arabella Greenville, and to converse freely with her at all proper times and seasons.

But that I know the very noble nature of my Grandmother, and am prepared, old as I am, to defend her fame even to taking the heart's blood of the villain that maligned her, I might blush at having to record a fact which must needs be set down here. Ere six months had passed, there grew up between Mrs. Greenville and the Prisoner a very warm and close friendship, which in time ripened into the tenderest of attachments. That her love for her dear Frank ever wavered, or that she ever swerved for one moment in her reverence for his memory, I cannot and I will not believe; but she nevertheless looked with an exceeding favour upon the imprisoned man, and made no scruple of avowing her Flame to Ruth. This young person did in time confide the same to her father, who was much concerned thereat, he not knowing how far the allowance of any love-passages between two such strangely assorted suitors might tally with his duty towards the King and Government. Nor could he shut his eyes to the fact that the Prisoner regarded Mrs. Greenville first with a tender compassion (such as a father might have towards his child), next with an ardent sympathy, and finally--and that very speedily too--with a Feeling that had all the Signs and Portents of Love. These two unfortunate People were so shut out from the world, and so spiritually wedded by a common Misery and discomfort, that their mere earthly coming together could not be looked upon but as natural and reasonable; for Mrs. Greenville was the only woman upon whom the Prisoner could be expected to look,--he being, beyond doubt, one of Gentle Degree, if not of Great and Noble Station, and therefore beyond aught but the caresses of a Patron with such a simple maid as Ruth Glover, whose father, although of some military rank, was, like most of the Captains who had served under the Commonwealth (witness Ireton, Harrison, Hacker, and many more) of exceeding mean extraction.

That love-vows were interchanged between this Bride and Bridegroom of Sorrow and a Dark Dungeon almost, I know not; but their liking for each other's society--he imparting to her some of his studies, and she playing music, with implements of which she was well provided, to him of an afternoon--had become so apparent both to the soldiers on guard and servants, even to the poor Invalid Matrosses wheezing and shivering in their buff-coats, that Colonel Glover, in a very flurry of uncertainty, sent post haste to Whitehall to know what he was to do--whether to chamber up Mrs. Greenville in her chamber, as of aforetime, or confine the Prisoner in one of the lower vaults in the body of the rock, with so many pounds weight of iron on his legs. For Colonel Glover was a man accustomed to use strong measures, whether with his family or with those he had custody over.

No answer came for many days; and the Governor had almost begun to think his message to be forgotten, when one summer evening (A.D. 1661) a troop of horse were seen galloping from the Village towards the Castle. The Drawbridge, which was on the ordinary kept slung, was now lowered; and the captain of the troop passing up to the barbican, gave Colonel Glover a sealed packet, and told him that he and his men would bivack at the bridge-foot (for the fens were passable at this season) until one who was expected at nightfall should come. Meat and drink were sent for, and the soldiers, dismounting, began to take tobacco and rail against the Castle in their brutal fashion--shame on them!--as an old mangy rat-trap.

Colonel Glover went up into his chamber in extreme disturbance. He had opened the packet and conned its contents; and having his daughter to him presently, and charging her, by her filial duty, to use discretion in all things that he should confide to her, tells her that his Majesty the King of England, France, and Ireland was coming to the Castle in a strictly Disguised habit that very evening.

There was barely time to make the slightest of preparations for this Glorious

Guest; but what there was, and of the best of Meat, and Wine, and Plate, and hangings, and candles in sconces, was set out in the Governor's chamber, and ordered as handsomely as might be for his Majesty's coming. About eight o'clock--the villagers being given to understand that only some noble commander is coming to pass the soldiers in the Castle in review--arrived two lackeys, with panniers and saddle-bags, and a French varlet, who said he was, forsooth, a cook, and carried about with him a whole elaboratory of stove-furnaces, pots and pans, and jars of sauces and condiments. Monsieur was quickly at work in the kitchen, turning all things topsy-turvy, and nearly frightening Margery, the old cook, who had been a baggage-wagon sutler at Naseby in the Great Wars, into fits. About half-past ten a trumpet was heard to wind at the bridge-foot, and a couple of horses came tramping over the planks, making the chains rattle even to the barbican, where their riders dismounted.

The King, for it is useless to make any further disguise about him--although the Governor deferred falling on his knees and kissing his hand until he had conducted him to his own chamber--was habited in strict incognito, with an uncurled wig, a flap-hat, and a horseman's coat over all. He had not so much as a hanger by his side, carrying only a stout oak walking-staff. With him came a great lord, of an impudent countenance, and with a rich dress beneath his cloak, who, when his Master was out of the room, sometimes joked with, and sometimes swore at, poor little Ruth, as, I grieve to say, was the uncivil custom among the Quality in those wild days. The King supped very copiously, drinking many beakers of wine, and singing French songs, to which the impudent Lord beat time, and sometimes presumed to join in chorus. But this Prince was ever of an easy manner and affable complexion, which so well explains the Love his people bore him. All this while the Governor and Ruth waited at table, serving the dishes and wine on their knees; for they would suffer no mean hirelings to wait upon their guests.

As the King drank--and he was a great taker of wine--he asked a multitude of questions concerning the Prisoner and Mrs. Greenville, to all of which Colonel Glover made answer in as plain a manner as was consistent with his deep loyalty and reverence. Soon, however, Colonel Glover found that his Majesty was paying far more attention to the bottle than to his conversation, and, about one in the morning, was conducted, with much reverence, to the Governor's own sleeping-chamber, which had been hastily prepared. His Majesty was quite Affable, but Haggard visibly. The impudent Lord was bestowed in the chamber which had been Ruth's, before she came to sleep so near Mrs. Greenville; and it is well he knew not what a pretty tenant the room had had, else would he have doubtless passed some villanous pleasantries thereupon.

The King, who was always an early riser, was up betimes in the morning; and on Colonel Glover representing to him his sorrow for the mean manner in which he had of necessity been lodged, answered airily that he was better off there than in the Oak, or in Holland, without a styver in his pocket; "Although, oddsfish!" quoth his Majesty, "this Castle of mine seems fitter to harbour wild-ducks than Christians." And then nothing would suit his Majesty but to be introduced to Mrs. Greenville, with whom he was closeted two whole hours.

He came forth from her chamber with his dark, saturnine face all flushed. "A brave woman!--a bold woman!" he kept saying. "An awful service she was like to have done me; and all to think that it was for love of poor Frank." For this Prince had known the Lord Francis well, and had shown him many favours.

"And now, good Master Governor," the King continued, but with quite another expression on his countenance, "we will see your Man Captive, if it shall so please you." And the two went upstairs.

This is all I am permitted to tell in this place of what passed between King Charles the Second and the Prisoner in the upper chamber:--

"You know me!" the King said, sitting over against him at the table, and scanning his face with dark earnestness.

"You are Charles Stuart, second of the name on the throne of England."

"You know I am in the possession of your secret--of the King's Secret; for of those dead it was known but to Oliver, as of those living it is now only known to yourself and to me."

"And the young Man, Richard?"

"He never knew it. His father never trusted him so far. He had doubts and suspicions, that was all."

"Thank God!" said the prisoner.

"What was Oliver's enmity towards you, that he should immure you here all these years?"

"I had served him too well. He feared lest the Shedder of Blood should become the Avenger of Blood."

"Are you sorry?"

"Sorry!" cried the Prisoner, with a kind of scream. "Had he a thousand lives, had I a thousand hands, I would do the same deed to-morrow." And he struck the right hand that was covered with the velvet glove with cruel violence on to the oaken table.

NOTES:

[I] A woman of very mean belongings, whose parents lived, I have heard, somewhere about the Maypole in the Strand, and who was promoted to high station, being Monk's Duchess, but to her death of a coarse and brutish carriage, and shamefully given to the drinking of strong waters.--J. D.

[J] A very glorious rag nevertheless.--ED.

CHAPTER THE SEVENTH.

I AM BRED UP IN VERY BAD COMPANY, AND (TO MY SHAME) HELP
TO KILL THE KING'S DEER.

I LAY all that night in a little Hole by the side of a Bank, just as though I had
been a Fox-cub. I was not in much better case than that Vermin, and I only
marvel that my Schoolmaster did not come out next day to Hunt me with
horses and hounds. Hounds!--the Black Fever to him!--he had used me like
a Hound any time for Six Months past; and often had I given tongue under his
Double Thonging. Happily the weather was warm, and I got no hurt by sleeping in
the Hole. 'Tis strange, too, what Hardships and Hazards of Climate and Excess we
can bear in our Youth, whereas in middle life an extra Slice gives us a Surfeit, and
another cup turns our Liver to Touchwood; whilst in age (as I know to my sorrow)
we dare scarcely venture our shoe in a Puddle for fear of the Chills and Sciatica. In
the morning I laved my face in a Brook that hurtled hard by; but waited very fear-
fully until Noon ere I dared venture forth from my covert. I had filled my pockets
with Fruit and Bread (which I am afraid I did not come very honestly by, and indeed admit that Gnawbit's Larder and Orchard found me in Provender), and was so
able to break my fast. And my Guinea, I remembered, was still unchanged. I had a
dim kind of impression that I was bound to Charlwood Chase, to join the Blacks of
whom the Old Gentleman had spoken, but I was not in any Hurry to get to my Goal.
I was Free, albeit a Runaway, and felt all the delights of Independence. You whose
pleasures lie in Bowers, and Beds, and Cards, and Wine, can little judge of the Ease
felt by him who is indeed a Beggar and pursued, but is at Liberty. I remember being
in hiding once with a Gentleman Robber, who had, by the aid of a File and a Friend,
contrived to give the Galleys leg-bail, and who for days afterwards was never tired

of patting and smoothing his ankles, and saying, "'Twas there the shackles galled me so." Poor rogue! he was soon afterwards laid by the heels and swung; for there is no Neck Verse in France to save a Gentleman from the Gallows.

Towards evening my gall began to grate somewhat with the sense of mine own utter loneliness; and for a moment I Wavered between the resolve to go Forward, and a slavish prompting to return to my Tyrant, and suffer all the torments his cruelty could visit me with. Then, as a middle course, I thought I would creep back to my kennel and die there; but I was happily dissuaded from such a mean surrender to Fortune's Spites through the all-unknowing agency of a Bull, that, spying me from afar off where he was feeding, came thundering across two fields and through a shallow stream, routed me up from my refuge, and chased me into the open. I have often since been thankful to this ungovernable Beast (that would have Tossed, and perchance Gored me sorely, had he got at me), and seldom, in later life, when I have felt weak and wavering in the pursuit of a profitable purpose, have I failed to remember the Bull, and how he chased me out of Distempered Idleness into Activity.

The Sun had begun to welk in the west by the time I had mustered up enough courage to come into the High Road, which I had an uncertain idea stretched away from Gnawbit's house, and towards Reading. But suddenly recalling the Danger of travelling by the Highway, where I might be met by Horsemen or Labouring persons sent in quest of me,--for it did not enter my mind that I was too worthless a scholar to be Pursued, and that Gnawbit was, 'tis likely enough, more Pleased than sorry to be Rid of me,--I branched off from the main to the left; so walking, as it seemed to me, many miles, I grew grievously hungry. No more Bread or Apples remained in my pouch; but I still had my Guinea, so I deemed, and resolved that if I came upon any House of Entertainment, I would sup. For indeed, while all Nature round me seemed to be taking some kind of Sustenance, it was hard that I, a Christian, should go to bed (or into another Fox-hole, for bed I had none, and yet had slept in my time in a grand chamber in Hanover Square) with an empty belly. The Earth was beginning to drink up the dews, like an insatiate toper as she is. I passed a flock of sheep biting their hasty supper from the grass; and each one with a little cloud of gnats buzzing around it, that with feeble stings, poor insects, were trying for their supper too. And 'tis effect we have upon another. The birds had taken home their worm-cheer to the little ones in the nests, and were singing their after-supper songs, very sweetly but drowsily. 'Twas too late in the year for the Nightingale,--that I knew,--but the jolly Blackbird was in full feather and voice; and presently there swept by me a great Owl, going home to feast, I will be bound, in his hollow tree, and with nothing less than a Field Mouse for his supper, the rascal. 'Twas a wicked imagining, but I could not help thinking, as I heard the birds carolling so merrily,--and how they keep so plump upon so little to eat is always to me a marvel, until I remember with what loving care Heaven daily spreads their table from Nature's infinite ordinary,--how choice a Refection a dish of birds' eggs, so often idly stolen and blown hollow by us boys, would make. The feathered creatures are a forgiving folk; and 'tis not unlikely that the Children in the Wood had often gone birds'-nesting: but when they were dead, the kindly Red Jerkins forgave all their little maraudings, and covered them with leaves, as though the children had strewn them crumbs or brought them worms from January to December. Gnawbit was a wretch who used to kill the Robins, and for that, if for naught else, he will surely howl.

By and by, when darkness was coming down like a playhouse curtain, and the Northern wagoner up yonder--how often have I watched him at sea!--was yoking his seven cart-mares to the steadfast star, I came upon a Man--the first I had seen since the Old Gentleman bade me begone with my Guinea, and join the Blacks. This Man was not walking or running, nay nor sitting nor lying as Lazars do in hedges. But he tumbled out of the quicket as it were, and came to me with short leaps, making as though he would Devour me. We schoolboys had talked often enough about Claude Duval and the Golden Farmer, and I set this Dreadful Being down at once as a Highwayman; so down I went Plump on my knees and Roared for mercy, as I was wont to do to Gnawbit, till I learnt that no Roaring would make him desist from his brutish purpose. It was darkish now, and I well-nigh fancied the Man was indeed my wicked Master, for he had an uplifted weapon in his hand; but when he came nearer to me, I found that it was not a cane nor a thong, but a Great Flail, which he whirled over his head, and then brought down on the ground with a Thwack, making the Night Flies dance.

"You Imp of mischief," said the man as he seized me by the collar and shook me roughly, "what are you doing here, spying on honest folks? Speak, or I'll brain you with this Flail."

I thought it best to tell this terrible man the Truth.

"If you please, sir," I answered, trembling, "I've run away."

"Run away from where, you egg?"

"From Gnawbit's, sir."

"And who the pest is Gnawbit, you hempen babe?"

"My schoolmaster, sir."

"Ha! that's good," the Man replied, loosening his hold somewhat on my collar. "And what did you run away for?"

I told him in broken sentences my short Story--of my Sufferings at School, at least, but never saying a word about my being a little Gentleman, and the son of a Lady of Quality in Hanover Square.

"And where are you going?" the Man asked, when I had finished.

I told him that I was on my way to Charlwood Chase to join the Blacks. And then he asked me whether I had any Money, whereto I answered that I had a Guinea; and little doubting in my Quaking Heart but that he would presently Wrench it from me, if haply he were not minded to have Meal as well as Malt, and brain me as he had threatened. But he forbore to offer me violence, and, quite releasing his hold, said--

"I suppose you'd like some supper."

I said that I had not broken my fast for many hours, and was dead a-hungered.

"And wouldn't mind supping with the Blacks in Charlwood Chase, eh?" he continued.

I rather gave him to understand that such was not only my Wish but my Ambition.

"Come along to the Blacks, then," said the Man. "I'm one of 'em."

He drew a Lantern from under his garments as he spoke, and letting out the Light from the slide, passed it over, and up and down, his Face and Figure. Then did I see with Horror and Amazement that both his Countenance and his Raiment were all smirched and bewrayed with dabs and patches of what seemed soot or blackened grease. It was a once white Smock or Gaberdine that made the chief part of his apparel; and this, with the black patches on it, gave him a Pied appearance fearful to behold. There was on his head what looked like a great bundle of black rags; and tufts of hair that might have been pulled out of the mane of a wild horse grew out from either side of his face, and wreathed its lower half.

"Come along," repeated the Man; "we'll blacken you bravely in time my Chicken-skin."

And so he grasped my hand in his,--and when I came to look at it afterwards, I found it smeared with sable, and with great black finger-marks upon it,--and led me away. We journeyed on in the Dark--for he had put up his Lantern--for another good half-hour, he singing to himself from time to time some hoarse catches of song having reference to some "Billy Boys" that I conjectured were his companions. And so we struck from by-lane into by-lane, and presently into a Plantation, and then through a gap in a Hedge, and through a Ditch full of Brambles, which galled my legs sorely. I was half asleep by this time, and was only brought to full wakefulness by the deep baying as of a Dog some few yards, as it seemed, from us.

The Lantern's light gleamed forth again; and in the circle of Clear it made I could see we were surrounded by tall Trees that with their long crooked Arms looked as though they would entwine me in deadly embraces.

"Hist!" the man said very low. "That's surely Black Towzer's tongue." And to my huge dismay he set up a sad responsive Howl, very like unto that of a Dog, but not at all akin to the voice of a Man.

The answer to this was a whistle, and human speech, saying--

"Black Jowler!"

"Black Towzer, for a spade Guinea!" my companion made answer; and in another moment there came bounding towards us another fellow in the same blackened masquerade as he, and with another Lantern. He had with him, besides, a shaggy hound that smelt me suspiciously and prowled round me, growling low, I shivering the whiles.

"What have we here?" asked the Second Black; for I made no doubt now but that my Company were of that Confederacy.

"Kid loose," replied he who was to take me to supper. "Given the keepers the slip, and run down by Billy Boys' park. Aha!" and he whispered to his comrade ruffian.

Out went the Lanterns again, and he who answered to the name of Jowler tightened his grasp, and bade me for a young Tyburn Token quicken my pace. So we walked and walked again, poor I as sore as a pilgrim tramping up the Hill to Louth--which I have many times seen in those parts--with Shards in his shoes. Then it must come, forsooth, to more whistling; and the same Play being over, we had one more Lantern to our Band, and one more Scurvy Companion as Black as a Flag,[K] who in their kennel Tongue was Mungo. And by and by we were joined by Surly, and Black Tom, and Grumps; and so with these five Men, who were pleased to be called as the Beasts are, I stumbled along, tired, and drowsy, and famishing, and thinking my journey would never come to an end.

Surely it must have been long past midnight when we made a halt; and all the five lanterns being lit, and making so many dancing wheels of yellow, I found that we were still encircled by those tall trees with the twining arms. And Jowler--for it is useless to speak of my conductor according to Human Rule--gave me a rough pat on the shoulder, and bade me cheer up, for that I should have my supper very soon now. All five then joined in a whistle so sharp, so clear, and so well sustained, that it sounded well-nigh melodious; and to this there came, after the lapse of a few seconds, the noise as of a little peevish Terrier barking.

"True as Touchwood," cried Black Jowler. "In, Billy Boys, and hey for fat and flagons."

With this he takes me by the shoulders, telling me to fear naught, and spend my money like a gentleman, and bundles me before him till we came to something hard as board. This I presently found was a door; and in an instant I was in the midst of a kind of Tavern parlour, all lighted up with great candles stuck into lumps of clay, and face to face with the Fattest Woman I ever saw in my life.

"Mother Moll Drum," quoth my conductor, "save you, and give me a quart of three threads, or I faint. Body o' me, was ever green plover so pulled as I was?"

The Fat Woman he called Mother Moll Drum was to all seeming in no very blessed temper; for she bade Jowler go hang for a lean polecat, and be cursed meanwhile, and that she would draw him naught.

"Come, come, Mother," Jowler said, making as though to appease her, "what be these tantrums? Come, draw; for I'm as thirsty as an hour-glass, poor wretch, that has felt sand run through his gullet any time these twenty years."

"Draw for yourself, rogue," says Mother Drum; "there's naught I'll serve you with, unless, indeed, I were bar-woman at St. Giles's Pound, and had to froth you your last quart, as you went up the Heavy Hill to Tyburn."

"We shall all go there in time--good time," breaks in a deep solemn voice, drawn somehow through the nose, and coming from the Man-Dog they called Grumps; "meanwhile, O greasy woman, let the beverage our brother asked for be drawn, and I, even Grumps, will partake thereof, and ask a blessing."

"Woman yourself!" cries Moll Drum, in a rage. "Woman yourself, and T---- in your teeth, and woman to the mother that bore you, and sat in the stocks for Lightness! Who are you, quotha, old reverend smock with the splay foot? Come up, now, prithee, Bridewell Bird! You will drink, will you? I saw no dust or cobwebs come out of your mouth. Go hang, you moon-calf, false faucet, you roaring horse-courser, you ranger of Turnbull, you dull malt-house with a mouth of a peck and the sign of the swallow above."

By this time Mother Drum was well-nigh out of breath, and panted, and looked so hot, that they might have put her up by Temple Bar on Queen Bess's birthnight for a Bonfire, and so saved Tar Barrels. And as she spoke she brandished a large Frying Pan, from which great drops of hot grease--smelling very savoury by the way--dropped on to the sanded floor. The other Blacks seemed in nowise disturbed by this Dispute, but were rather amused thereby, and gathered in a ring round Jowler and Grumps and the Fat Woman, laughing.

"Never mind, Mother Drum," quoth one; "she was a pig-woman once in Bartle-my Fair, and lost her temper through the heat of a coal-fire roasting porkers. Was't not hot, Mother Drum? was not Tophet a kind of cool cellar to it?"

It was Surly who spoke, and Mother Drum turns on him in a rage.

"You lie, you pannierman's by-blow!" she cried; "you bony muckfowl, with the bony back sticking out like the ace of spades on the point of a small-sword! you lie, Bobchin, Changeling, Horseleech! 'Slid, you Shrovetide Cutpurse, I'll scald your hide with gravy, I will!"

"Ware the pan, ware the pan!" all the Blacks cried out; for the Good Woman made a flourish as though she would have carried out her threat; whereupon my Man-Dog, Jowler, thought it was time to interpose, and spoke.

"There's no harm in Mother Drum, but that her temper's as hot as her pan, and we are late to supper. Come, Mother, Draw for us, and save you still. I'll treat you to burnt brandy afterwards."

"What did he call me Pig-Woman for?" she grumbled, but still half mollified. "What if I did waste my youth and prime in cooking of porkers in a booth; I am no cutpurse. I, I never shoved the tumbler for tail-drawing or poll-snatching on a levee-day.[L] But I will draw for you, and welcome my guests of the game."

"And Supper, good Moll, Supper," added Jowler.

"An you had not hindered me, it would have been ready upstairs. There are more upstairs besides you that hunger after the fat and the lean. But can you sup without a cook? Will venison run off the spit ready roasted, think you, like the pigs in Lubberland, that jump down your throat, and cry *wee wee*?"

She began to bustle about, and summoned, by the name of Cicely Grip--adding thereto the epithet of "faggot"--a stout serving-lass, who might have been comely enough, but whose face and hands were very nearly as black as those of the Man-Dog's. This wench brought a number of brown jugs full of beer, and the Blacks took to drinking with much zest. Then Jowler, who seemed a kind of lieutenant, in some authority over them, gave the word of command to "Peel;" and they hastened to leave the room, which was but a mean sort of barn-like chamber, with bare walls, a wattled roof, and a number of rough wooden tables and settles, all littered with jugs and Tobacco pipes. So I and the Fat Woman and Jowler, Cicely Grip having betaken herself to the kitchen, were left together.

"Cicely will dish up, Mother Drum," he says; "you have fried collops enow for us, I trow; and if more are wanted for the Billy Boys, you can to your pan again. You began your brandy pottage too early tonight, Mother. Let us have no more of your vapours 'twixt this and day-break, prithee. What would Captain Night say?"

"Captain Night be hanged!"

"He will be hanged, as our brother Surly has it, in good time, I doubt it not. Meanwhile, order must be kept at the Stag o' Tyne. Get you and draw the dram I promised you; and, Mother, wash me this little lad's face and hands, that he may sit down to meat with us in a seemly manner."

"Who the Clink is he?" asked Mother Drum, eyeing me with no very Great Favour.

"He says he is little Boy Jack," answered Mr. Jowler, gravely. "We will give him another name before we have done with him. Meantime he has a guinea in his pocket to pay his shot, and that's enough for the fat old Alewife of the Stag o'

Tyne."

"Fat again!" muttered Mother Drum. "Is it a 'Sizes matter to be full of flesh? I be fat indeed," she answered, with a sigh, "and must have a chair let out o' the sides for me, that these poor old hips may have play. And I, that was of so buxom a figure."

"Never mind your Figure, Mother," remarked my Conductor, "but do my bidding. I'll e'en go and peel too;" and without more ado he leaves us.

Madam Drum went into her kitchen and fetched forth a Tin Bowl full of hot suds, and with these she washed me as she had been directed. I bore it all unresistingly--likewise a scrubbing with a rough towel. Then, when my hair was kempt with an old Felting comb, almost toothless, I felt refreshed and hungrier than ever. But Mother Drum never ceased to complain of having been called fat.

"Time was, my smooth-faced Coney," she said, "that I was as lithe and limber as you are, and was called Jaunty Peg. And now poor old Moll cooks collops for those that are born to dance jigs in chains for the north-east wind to play the fiddle to. Time was when a whole army followed me, when I beat the drum before the great Duke."

"What Duke?" I asked, looking up at her great red face.

"What Duke, milksop! Why, who should I mean but the Duke that won Hochstedt and Ramilies:--the Ace of Trumps, my dear, that saved the Queen of Hearts, the good Queen Anne, so bravely. What Duke should I mean but John o' Marlborough."

"I have seen *him*," I said, with childish gravity.

"Seen him! when and where, loblolly-boy? You're too young to have been a drummer."

"I saw him," I answered, blushing and stammering; "I saw him when--when I was a little Gentleman."

"Lord save us!" cries Mother Drum, bursting into a jolly laugh. "A Gentleman! since when, your Lordship, I pray? But we're all Gentlefolks here, I trow; and Captain Night's the Marquis of Aylesbury Jail. A Gentleman! oho!"

Hereupon, and which, to my great relief, quitted me of the perturbation brought on by a Rash Admission, there came three knocks from above, and Mother Drum said hurriedly, "Supper, supper;" and opening a side-door, pushes me on to a staircase, and tells me to mount, and pull a reverence to the company I found at table.

Twenty steps brought me to another door I found on the jar, and I passed into a great room with a roof of wooden joists, and a vast table in the middle set out with supper. There was no table-cloth; but there were plenty of meats smoking hot in great pewter dishes. I never saw, either, so many bottles and glasses on one board in my life; and besides these, there was good store of great shining Flagons, carved and chased, which I afterwards knew to be of Solid Silver.

Round this table were gathered at least Twenty Men; and but for their voices I should never have known that five among them were my companions of just now. For all were attired in a very brave Manner, wore wigs and powder and embroidered waistcoats; although, what I thought strange, each man dined in boots, with a gold-laced hat on his head, and his Hanger by his side, and a brace of Pistols on the table beside him. Yet I must make two exceptions to this rule. He whom they called Surly, had on a full frizzed wig and a cassock and bands, that, but for his rascal face, would have put me in mind of the Parson at St. George's, Hanover Square, who always seemed to be so angry with me. Surly was Chaplain, and said Grace, and ate and drank more than any one there. Lastly, at the table's head, sat a thin, pale, proper kind of a man, wearing his own hair long, in a silken club, dressed in the pink of Fashion, as though he were bidden to a birthday, with a dandy rapier at his side, and instead of Pistols, a Black Velvet Visor laid by the side of his plate. He had very large blue eyes and very fair hair. He might have been some thirty-five years old, and the guests, who treated him with much deference, addressed him as Captain Night.

Mr. Jowler, whose hat had as brave a cock as any there, made me sit by him; and, with three more knocks and the Parson's Grace, we all fell to supper. They helped me plentifully, and I ate my fill. Then my friend gave me a silver porringer full of wine-and-water. It was all very good; but I knew not what viands I was eating, and made bold to ask Jowler.

"'Tis venison, boy, that was never shot by the King's keeper," he answered. "But, if you would be free of Charlwood Chase, and wish to get out yet with a whole skin, I should advise you to eat your meat and ask no questions."

I was very much frightened at this, and said no more until the end of Supper. When they had finished, they fell to drinking of Healths, great bowls of Punch being brought to them for that purpose. The first toast was the King, and that fell to

Jowler.

"The King!" says he, rising.

"Over the water?" they ask.

"No," answers Jowler. "The King everywhere. King James, and God bless him."

"I won't drink *that*," objects the Chaplain. "You know I am a King George man."

"Drink the Foul Fiend, an' you will," retorts the Proposer. "You'd be stanch and true either way. Now, Billy Boys, the King!"

And they fell to tumbling down on their knees, and drinking His Majesty in brimming bumpers. I joined in the ceremony perforce, although I knew nothing about King James, save that Monarch my Grandmother used to Speak about, who Withdrew himself from these kingdoms in the year 1688; and at Church 'twas King George they were wont to pray for, and not King James. And little did I ween that, in drinking this Great Person on my knees, I was disobeying the Precept of my dear dead Kinswoman.

"I have a bad foot," quoth Captain Night, "and cannot stir from my chair; but I drink all healths that come from loyal hearts."

Many more Healths followed. The Chaplain gave the Church, "and confusion to Old Rapine, that goes about robbing chancels of their chalices, and parsons of their dues, and the very poor-box of alms." And then they drank, "Vert and Venison," and then, "A black face, a white smock, and a red hand." And then they betook themselves to Roaring choruses, and Smoking and Drinking galore, until I fell fast asleep in my chair.

I woke up not much before Noon the next day, in a neat little chamber very cleanly appointed; but found to my surprise that, in addition to my own clothes, there was laid by my bedside a little Smock or Gaberdine of coarse linen, and a bowl full of some sooty stuff that made me shudder to look at. And my Surprise was heightened into amazed astonishment when, having donned my own garments, and while curiously turning over the Gaberdine, there came a knock, and anon stepped into the room the same comely Servant-maid that had ridden with us in the Wagon six months since, on that sad journey to school, and that had been so kind to me in the way of new milk and cheesecakes.

She was very smartly dressed, with a gay flowered apron, and a flycap all over glass-beads, like so many Blue-bottles. And she had a gold brooch in her stomacher, and fine thread hose, and red Heels to her shoes.

She was as kind to me as ever, and told me that I was among those who would treat me well, and stand my friends, if I obeyed their commands. And I, who, I confess, had by this time begun to look on the Blacks and their Ways with a kind of Schoolboy glee, rose, nothing loth, and donned the Strange Accoutrements my entertainers provided for me. The girl helped me to dress, smiling and giggling mightily the while; but, as I dressed, I could not help calling her by the name she had given me in the Wagon, and asking how she had come into that strange Place.

"Hush, hush!" says she. "I'm Marian now, Maid Marian, that lives with Mother Drum, and serves the Gentlemen Blacks, and brings Captain Night his morning Draught. None of us are called by our real names at the Stag o' Tyne, my dear. We all are in No-man's-land."

"But where is No-man's-land, and what is the Stag o' Tyne?" I asked, as she slipped the Gaberdine over my head.

"No-man's-land is just in the left-hand top Corner of Charlwood Chase, after you have turned to the left, and gone as far forward as you can by taking two steps backward for every one straight on," answers the saucy hussy. "And the Stag o' Tyne's even a Christian House of Entertainment that Mother Drum keeps."

"And who is Mother Drum?" I resumed, my eyes opening wider than ever.

"A decent Alewife, much given to grease, and that cooks the King's Venison for Captain Night and his Gentlemen Blacks."

"And Captain Night,--who is he?"

"Ask me no questions, and I'll tell you no lies," she makes reply. "Captain Night is a Gentleman every inch of him, and as sure as Tom o' Ten Thousand."

"And the Gentlemen Blacks?"

"Your mighty particular," quoth she, regarding me with a comical look. "Well, my dear, since you are to be a Black yourself, and a Gentleman to boot, I don't mind telling you. The Gentlemen Blacks are all Bold Hearts, that like to kill the King's Venison without a Ranger's Warrant, and to eat of it without paying Fee nor Royalty, and that drink of the very best--"

"And that have Dog-whips to lay about the shoulders of tattling minxes and curious urchins," cries, to my dismay, a voice behind us, and so to us--by his voice at least--Captain Night, but in his body no longer the same gay spark that I had seen the night before, or rather that morning early. He was as Black, and Hairy, and Savage-looking as any--as Jowler, or any one of that Dark Gang; and in no way differed from them, save that on the middle finger of his Right Hand there glittered from out all his Grease and Soot, a Great Diamond Ring.

"Come," he cries, "Mistress Nimble Tongue, will you be giving your Red Rag a gallop yet, and Billy Boys waiting to break their Fast? Despatch, and set out the boy, as I bade you."

"I am no kitchen-wench, I," answers the Maid of the Wagon, tossing her head. "Cicely o' the Cinders yonder will bring you to your umble-pie, and a Jack of small-beer to cool you, I trow. Was it live Charcoal or Seacoal embers that you swallowed last night, Captain, makes you so dry this morning?"

"Never mind, Goody Slack Jaw," says Captain Night. "I shall be thirstier anon from listening to your prate. Will you hurry now, Gadfly, or is the sun to sink before we get hounds in leash?"

Thus admonished, the girl takes me by the arm, and, without more ado, dips a rag in the pot of black pigment, and begins to smear all my hands, and face, and throat, with dabs of disguising shade. And, as she bade me do the same to my Garment, and never spare Soot, I fell to work too, making myself into the likeness of a Chimney-boy, till they might have taken me into a nursery to Frighten naughty children.

Captain Night sat by himself on the side of the bed, idly clicking a pistol-lock till such time as he proceeded to load it, the which threw me into a cold tremor, not knowing but that it might be the Custom among the Gentlemen Blacks to blow out the brains in the morning of those they had feasted over-night. Yet, as there never was Schoolboy, I suppose, but delighted in Soiling of his raiment, and making himself as Black as any sweep in Whetstone Park, so did I begin to feel something like a Pleasure in being masqueraded up to this Disguise, and began to wish for a Pistol such as Captain Night had in his Hand, and such a Diamond Ring as he wore on his finger.

"There!" cries the Maid of the Wagon, when I was well Blacked, surveying me approvingly. "You're a real imp of Charlwood Chase now. Ugh! thou young Rig!

I'll kiss you when the Captain brings you home, and good soap and water takes off those mourning weeds before supper-time."

She had clapped a great Deerskin cap on my head, and giving me a friendly pat, was going off, when I could not help asking her in a sly whisper what had become of the Pewterer of Pannier Alley.

"What! you remember him, do you?" she returned, with a half-smile and a half-sigh. "Well, the Pewterer's here, and as black as you are."

"But I thought you were to wed," I remarked.

"Well!" she went on, almost fiercely, "cannot one wed at the Stag o' Tyne? We have a brave Chaplain down-stairs,--as good as a Fleet Parson any day, I wuss."

"But the Pewterer?" I persisted.

"I'll hang the Pewterer round thy neck!" she exclaimed in a pet. "The Pewterer was unfortunate in his business, and so took to the Road; and thus we have all come together in Charlwood Chase. But ask me no more questions, or Captain Night will be deadly angry. Look, he fumes already."

She tripped away saying this, and in Time, I think; for indeed the Captain was beginning to show signs of impatience. She being gone, he took me on his knee, all Black as I was, and in a voice kind enough, but full of authority, bade me tell him all my History and the bare truth, else would he have me tied neck and heels and thrown to the fishes.

So I told this strange Man all:--of Hanover Square, and my earliest childhood. Of the Unknown Lady, and her Behaviour and conversation, even to her Death. Of her Funeral, and the harsh bearing of Mistress Talmash and the Steward Cadwallader unto me in my Helplessness and Loneliness. Of my being smuggled away in a Wagon and sent to school to Gnawbit, and of the Barbarous cruelty with which I had been treated by that Monster. And finally, of the old Gentleman that used to cry, "Bear it! Bear it!" and of his giving me a Guinea, and bidding me run away.

He listened to all I had to say, and then putting me down,

"A strange story," he thoughtfully remarks, "and not learnt out of the story-books either, or I sorely err. You have not a Lying Face, my man. Wait a while, and you'll wear a Mask thicker than all that screen of soot you have upon you now." But in this he was mistaken; for John Dangerous ever scorned deception, and through life has always acted fair and above-board.

"And that Guinea," he continued. "Hast it still?"

I answered that I had, producing it as I spoke, and that I was ready to pay my Reckoning, and to treat him and the others, in which, meseems, there spoke less of the little Runaway Schoolboy that had turned Sweep, than of the Little Gentleman that was wont to be a Patron to his Grandmother's lacqueys in Hanover Square.

"Keep thy piece of Gold," he answers, with a smile. "Thou shalt pay thy footing soon enough. Or wilt thou go forth with thy Guinea and spend it, and be taken by thy Schoolmaster to be whipped, perchance to death?"

I replied that I had the much rather stay with him, and the Gentlemen.

"The less said of the 'Gentlemen' the better. However, 'tis all one: we are all Gentlemen at the Stag o' Tyne. Even thou art a Gentleman, little Ragamuff."

"I am a Gentleman of long descent; and my fathers have fought and bled for the True King; and Norman blood's better than German puddle-mud," I replied, repeating well-nigh Mechanically that which my dear Kinswoman had said to me, and Instilled into me many and many a time. In my degraded Slavery, I had *well*-nigh forgotten the proud old words; but only once it chanced that they had risen up unbidden, when I was flouted and jeered at as Little Boy Jack by my schoolmates. Heaven help us, how villanously cruel are children to those who are of their own age and Poor and Friendless! What is it that makes young hearts so Hard? The boys Derided and mocked me more than ever for that I said I was a Gentleman; and by and by comes Gnawbit, and beats me black and blue--ay, and gory too--with a furze-stub, for telling of Lies, as he falsely said, the Ruffian.

"Well," resumed Captain Night, "thou shalt stay with us, young Gentleman. But weigh it soberly, boy," he continued. "Thou art old enough to know black from white, and brass from gold. Be advised; know what we Blacks are. We are only Thieves that go about stealing the King's Deer in Charlwood Chase."

I told him that I would abide by him and his Company; and with a grim smile he clapped me on the shoulder, and told me that now indeed I was a Gentleman Black, and Forest Free.

NOTES:
[K] "My Flag" in the original MS.; but I put it down as a slip of the pen, and altered it--G. A. S.

[L] Madam Drum, so far as I can make out the **argot** of the day, here insinuated that her opponent had been corrected at the cart's tail for stealing swords out of the scabbards, and conveying wigs from the heads of their owners, two crimes which have become obsolete since the Quality have ceased to wear swords and periwigs.--G. A. S.

CHAPTER THE EIGHTH.

THE HISTORY OF MOTHER DRUM.

URING the long nights I remained at the Stag o' Tyne ere I was thought Worthy to join the Blacks in their nocturnal adventures, or was, by my Hardihood and powers of Endurance--poor little mite that I was--adjudged to be Forest Free, I remained under the charge of Ciceley of the Cindery, and of the corpulent Tapstress whom the Blacks called Mother Drum. These two women were very fond of gossiping with me; and especially did Mother Drum love to converse with me upon her own Career, which had been of the most Chequered, not to say Amazing nature. I have already hinted that at one time this Remarkable Woman had professed the Military Profession, in which she had shone with almost a Manly Brilliance; and from her various confidences--all delivered to me as they were in shreds and patches, and imparted at the oddest times and seasons--I was enabled to shape her (to me) diverting history into something like the following shape.

"I was born, I think," quoth Mother Drum, "in the year 1660, being that of his happy Restoration to the throne of these Realms of his late Sacred Majesty King Charles the Second. My father was a small farmer, who fed his pigs and tended his potato gardens at the foot of the Wicklow Mountains, about twelve miles from the famous city of Dublin. His name was O' something, which it concerns you not to know, youngster, and he had the misfortune to be a Papist. I say the misfortune; for in those days, O well-a-day, as in these too, and more's the shame, to be a Papist meant being a poor, unfortunate creature continually Hunted up and down, Harassed and Harried far worse than any leathern-skinned Beast of Venery that the Gentlemen Blacks pursue in Charlwood Chase. He had suffered much under the iron rule" (these were not exactly Mother Drum's words, for her language was anything, as a rule, but well chosen; but I have polished up her style a little,) "of the cruel Usurper, Oliver Cromwell; that is to say the Redcoated Ironsides of that Bad Man had on three several occasions burnt his Shelling to the ground, stolen his Pigs, and grubbed up his potato ground. Once had they ran away with his wife, (my dear Mother), twice had they half-hanged him to a tree-branch, and at divers intervals had they tortured him by tying lighted matches between his fingers. When, however, His Sacred Majesty was happily restored there were hopes that the poor Romanists would enjoy a little Comfort and Tranquillity; but these Fond aspirations were speedily and cruelly dashed to the ground; for the Anglican Bishops and Clergy being put into possession of the Sees and Benefices of which they had been so long deprived, occupied themselves much more with Hounding Down those who did not live by the Thirty-nine Articles and the Liturgy, than in preaching Peace and Goodwill among all men. So the Papists had a worse time of it than ever. My Father, honest man, tried to temporise between the two parties, but was ever in danger of being shot by his own friends as a Traitor, even if he escaped half-hanging at the hands of the Protestants as a Recusant. Well, after all, Jack high or Jack low, the days must come to an end, and Spring, Summer, Autumn, and Winter must follow upon one another, and boys and girls were born to my father, and the pigs littered, and were sold at market, and the potatoes grew and were eaten whether Oliver Cromwell, or his son Dickon, or Charles Stuart--I beg pardon, His Sacred Majesty-- was uppermost. Thus it was I came into the world in the Restoration year.

"I was a bold, strapping, fearless kind of a girl, much fonder of Romping and Horse-play of the Tomboy order than of the Pursuits and Pastimes of my own sex. The difference was more remarkable, as you know the Irish girls are distinguished above all other Maidens in creation by an extreme Delicacy and Coyness, not to say Prudishness of Demeanour. But Betty--I was christened Elizabeth--was always gammocking and tousling with the Lads instead of holding by her Mother's apron, or demurely sitting by her spinning-wheel, or singing plaintive ballads to herself to the music of the Irish Harp, which, in my time, almost every Farmer's Daughter could Play. Before I was seven years old I could feed the pigs and dig up the potato ground. Before I was ten, I could catch a colt and ride him, barebacked and without bridle, holding on by his mane, round the green in front of my Father's Homestead.

Before I was twelve, I was a match for any Boy of my own age at a bout of fisticuffs, ay, and at swinging a blackthorn so as to bring it down with a thwack on the softest part of a gossoon's crown. I knew little of spinning, or playing, or harping; but I could land a trout, and make good play with a pike. I could brew a jug of Punch, and at a jig could dance down the lithest gambriler of those parts, Dan Meagher, the Blind Piper of Swords. Those who knew me used to call me 'Brimstone Betty;' and in my own family I went by the name of the 'Bold Dragoon,' much to the miscontentment of my father, who tried hard to bring me to a more feminine habit of Body and frame of mind, both by affectionate expostulation, and by assiduous larruping with a stirrup leather. But 'twas all of no use. At sixteen I was the greatest Tearcoat of the Country side; and Father Macanasser, the village priest, gave it as his opinion that I must either be married, or sent to Dublin into decent service, or go to Ruination.

"It chanced that one fine summer day, I was gammocking in a hayfield with another lass, a friend of mine, whom I had made almost as bold as myself. We had a cudgel apiece, and were playing at single-stick, in our mad-cap fashion, laughing and screaming like Bedlamites, meanwhile. Only a hedge separated us from the high-road to Dublin, which ran up hill, and by and by came toiling up the hill, sticking every other minute in a rut, or jolting into a hole--for the roads were in infamous condition about here, as, indeed, all over the kingdom of Ireland--a grand coach, all over painting and gilding, drawn by six grey horses, with flowing manes and tails. The two leading pair had postilions in liveries of blue and silver, and great badges of coats-of-arms, and the equipage was further attended by a couple of outriders or yeomen-prickers in the same rich livery, but with cutlasses at their sides, petronels in their holsters, and blunderbusses on their hips, to guard against Tories and Rapparees, who then infested the land, and cared little whether it was Daylight or Moonlight--whether it was in the Green tree or the Dry that they went about their thievish business. The personage to whom this grand coach belonged was a stout, Majestic old Gentleman with a monstrous black periwig, a bright star on his breast, and a broad blue ribbon crossing his plum-coloured velvet doublet. He had dismounted from his heavy coach, while the horses were fagging up hill, and by the help of a great crutch-staff of ebony, ornamented with silver, was toiling after them. Hearing our prattling and laughing, he looked over the hedge and saw us in the very thick of our mimic Combat. This seemed to divert him exceedingly; and although we, seeing so grand a gentleman looking at us, were for suspending our Tomfoolery, and stood, to say the truth, rather shamefaced than otherwise among the haycocks, he bade us with cheery and encouraging words to proceed, and laughed to see us so sparring at one another, till his sides shook again. But all the fire was taken out of our combat, by the presence of so unwonted a Spectator, and after a brief lapse we dropped cudgels, and stood staring and blushing, quite dashed and confused. Then he beckoned us towards him in a most affable manner, and we came awkwardly and timorously, yet still with great curiosity to know what was to follow, through a gap in the hedge, and so stood before him in the road. And then cries out one of the Yeomen-Prickers--'Wenches! drop your best curtsey to his Grace the Duke of O----.' It was, indeed, that famous nobleman, lately Lord Lieutenant, and still one of the highest, mightiest, and most puissant Princes in the Kingdom of Ireland. To be brief, he put a variety of questions to us, respecting our belongings, and at my answers seemed most condescendingly pleased, and at those of my playmate (whose name was Molly O'Flaherty, and who had red hair, and a cast in her eye), but moderately pleased. On her, therefore, he bestowed a gold piece, and so dismissed her; telling her to take care of what her Tom Boy pranks might lead her to. But to me, while conferring the like present, he was good enough to say that I was a spirited lass fit for better things, and that if my Father and Mother would bring me shortly to his House in Dublin, he would see what could be done, to the end of bettering my condition in life. Whereupon he was assisted to his seat by one of four running footmen that tramped by his side, and away he went in his coach and six, leaving me in great joy and contentment. In only a few minutes came after him, not toiling, but bursting up the hill, a whole plump of gallant cavaliers in buff coats, bright corslets, and embroidered bandoliers over them, wearing green plumes in their hats, and flourishing their broadswords in the sunshine. These were the gentlemen of his bodyguard. They questioned me as to my converse with his Grace, and when I told them, laughed and said that I was in luck.

"The Duke of O---- meant me no harm, and I am sure did me none; and yet, my dear, I must date all my misfortunes from the time I was introduced to his Grace. You see that these gentlefolks have so much to think of, and are not in the habit of troubling their heads much as to what becomes of a poor peasant girl, after the whim which may have led them to patronize her has once passed over. My mother made me a new linsey woolsey petticoat, and a snood of scarlet frieze, and I was as fine as ninepence, with the first pair of stockings on that ever I had worn in my life, when I was taken to Dublin to a grand house by the Quay side, to be presented to his Grace. He had almost forgotten who I was, when his Groom of the Chamber procured us an audience. Then he remembered how he had laughed at my gambols with Molly O'Flaherty in the hayfield, and how they amused him, and how he thought my Romping ways might divert My Lady Duchess his Consort, who was a pining, puling, melancholic Temperament, and much afflicted with the Vapours, for want of something to do. So he was pleased to smile upon me again, and to give my mother five pounds, and to promise that I should be well bestowed in his household as a waiting-woman, or Bower-maiden, or some such like capacity; and then he made me a present, as though I were a puppy-dog, to Her Grace the Duchess, and having affairs of state to attend to, thought no more about 'Brimstone Betty.' My sprightly ways and random talk amused her Grace for awhile; but she had too many gewgaws and playthings, and I found, after not many days, that my popularity was on the wane, and that I could not hope to maintain it against the attractions of a French waiting-maid, a monkey, a parrot, a poodle, and a little Dwarfish boy-attendant that was half fiddler and half buffoon. So my consequence faded and faded, and I was sneered at and flouted as a young Savage and a young Irish by the English lacqueys about the House, and I sank from my Lady's keeping-room to the antechamber, and thence to the servant's hall, and thence, after a very brief lapse, to the kitchen, where I was very little better than a Scullish and Plate-washer, and not half so well entreated as Cicely of the Cinders is here. I pined and fretted; but time went on, and to my misfortune I was growing taller and shapelier. I had a very clear skin, and very black hair and eyes, and, though I say it that shouldn't, as neat a leg and foot as you would wish to see in a summer's day, and the men folk told me that I was comely. They only told me so, the false perfidious hounds, for my destruction.

"Well, child, you are too young to understand these things; and I hope that when you grow up, you will not do to poor forlorn girls as I was done by. A dicing soldier fellow that was a hanger-on at my Lord Duke's house, and was called Captain, ran away with me. Of course I was at once discarded from the Great House as a good-for-nothing Light o' love, and was told that if ever I presumed to show my face on the Quay-side again I should be sent to the Spinning House, and whipped. They had better have taken care of me while I was with them. The Captain dressed me up in fine clothes for a month or so, and gave me paint and patches, and took me to the Playhouse with a mask on, and then he got stabbed in a broil after some gambling bout at a China House in Smock Alley, and I was left in the wide world with two satin sacques, a box of cosmetiques, a broken fan, two spade guineas, and little else besides what I stood upright in. Return to my Father and Mother I dared not; for I knew that the tidings of my misconduct had already been conveyed to them, and had half broken their hearts, and my offence was one that is unpardonable in the children of the poorest and humblest of the Irishry. There was Bitter Bread before me, if I chose to follow, as thousands of poor, cozened, betrayed creatures before me had done, a Naughty Life; but this, with unutterable Loathing and Scorn, I cast away from me; and having, from my Dare-devil Temper, a kind of Pride and High Stomach made me determine to earn my livelihood in a bold and original manner. They had taught me to read at the Great House (though I knew not great A from a bowl's foot when I came into it) and so one of the first things I had spelt out was a chap-book ballad of Mary Ambree, the female soldier, that was at the siege of Ghent, and went through all the wars in Flanders in Queen Bess's time. 'What woman has done, woman can do,' cries I to myself, surveying my bold and masculine lineaments, my flashing black eyes, and ruddy tint, my straight, stout limbs, and frank, dashing gait. Ah! I was very different to the fat, pursy, old ale-wife who discourses with you now--in the glass. Without more ado I cut off my long black hair close to my head, stained my hands with walnut juice, (for they had grown white and soft and plump from idling about in the Great House), and went off to a Crimp in the Liberty that was enlisting men (against the law, but here many things are done against both Law and Prophets), for the King of France's service.

"This was in the year '80, and I was twenty years of age. King Louis had then no especial Brigade of Irish Troops--that famous corps not being formed until after the Revolution--and his Scotch Guards, a pinchbeck, purse-proud set of beggarly cavaliers, would not have any Irishry among them. I scorned to deny my lineage, and indeed my tongue would have soon betrayed me, had I done so; and the name I listed under was that of James Moriarty. One name is as good as another when you are going to the wars; and no name is, perchance, the best of any. As James Moriarty, after perfecting myself in musket-drill, and the pike-exercise, in our winter quarters at Dunkirk, I was entered in the Gardes Francais, a portion of the renowned Maison du Roy, or Household Troops, and as such went through the second Rhenish campaign, taking my share, and a liberal one too, in killing my fellow-Christians, burning villages, and stealing poultry. Nay, through excessive precaution, lest my sex should be discovered, I made more pretensions than the rest of my Comrades to be considered a lady-killer, and the Captain of my Company, Monsieur de la Ribaldiere, did me the honour to say that no Farmer's Daughter was safe from 'Le Bel Irlandais,' or Handsome Irishman, as they called me. Heaven help us! From whom are the Farmer's daughters, or the Farmers themselves safe in war time?

"When peace was declared, I found that I had risen to the dignity of Sergeant, and carried my Halberd with an assured strut and swagger, nobody dreaming that I was a wild Irish girl from the Wicklow Mountains. I might have risen, in time, to a commission and the Cross of St. Louis; but the piping times of peace turned all such brave grapes sour. I was glad enough, when the alternative was given me, of accompanying my Captain, Monsieur de la Ribaldiere, to Paris, as his Valet de Chambre, or of mouldering away, without hope of Promotion, in some country barrack, to choose the former, and led, for a year or two, a gay, easy life enough in the French Capital. But, alas! that which I had hidden from a whole army in the field, I could not keep a secret from one rubbishing, penniless, popinjay of a Captain in the Gardes Francaises. I told this miscreant, de la Ribaldiere, that I was a woman; for I was mad and vain enough to Love him. These are matters again, child, that you cannot understand; but I have said enough when I declare that if ever there was power in the Curse of Cromwell to blight a Wicked Man, that curse ought to light upon Henri de la Ribaldiere.

"I took a disgust to the male attire after this; but being yet in the prime of my womanhood, and as fond as ever of athletic diversions, I engaged myself to a French mountebank posture-master to dance Corantoes on the Tight and Slack Rope, accompanying myself meanwhile by reveilles on the Drum, an instrument in which I had become a proficient. The Posture Master, finding out afterwards that I was agile and Valiant, not only at Dancing but at Fighting, must needs have me wield the broadsword and the quarterstaff against all comers on a public platform; and, as the Irish Amazon, I achieved great success, and had my Employer not been a thief, should have gained much money. He was in the habit, not only of robbing his woman-performers, but of beating them; but I promise you the first time the villain offered to slash at me with his dog-whip, I had him under the jaw with my fist in the handsomest manner, and then tripping up his heels, and hurling him down on his own stage, and (having a right piece of ashplant in my grip) I did so curry his hide in sight of a full audience, that he howled for mercy, and the groundlings, who thought it part of the show, clapped their hands till they were sore and shouted till they were hoarse. Our engagement came to an end after this, and in a somewhat disagreeable manner for me; for the Posture-Master happened to be the by-blow of a Doctor of the Sorbonne, who was brother to an Abbe, who was brother to an opera-dancer, who had interest with a cardinal, who was uncle to a gentleman of the Chamber, who was one of Pere la Chaise's pet penitents; and this Reverend Father, having the King's ear, denounced me to his Majesty as a Spy, a Heretic, a Jansenist, a **Coureuse**, and all sorts of things; and by a **lettre de Cachet**, as they call their warrants, I was sent off to the prison of the Madelonettes, there to diet on bread and water, to be herded with the vilest of my sex, to card wool, and to receive, morning and evening, the Discipline (as they call it) of Leathern thongs, ten to a handful, and three blood-knots in each. I grew sick of being tawed for offences I had never committed, and so made bold one morning to try and strangle the Mother of the Workroom, who sat over us with a rattan, while we carded wool. Upon which I was bound to a post, and received more stripes, my lad, in an hour than ever your Schoolmaster gave you in a week. That same night I tried to burn the prison down; and then they put me in the dark dungeon called La Grande Force, with six inches of water in it and any number of rats. I was threatened with prosecution at their old Bailey, or Chatelet, with the Question (that is, the torture) ordinary and extraordinary, with the galleys for life as a wind-up, even if I escaped the gibbet in the place de Greve. Luckily for me, at this time the Gentleman of the Chamber fell into disgrace with Father la Chaise for eating a Chicken Sausage in Lent; and to spite him and the Minister, and the Cardinal and the Opera Dancer, and the Abbe and the Doctor of the Sorbonne, and the Posture Master all together, His Reverence, having his Majesty's ear, moves the Most Christian King to Clemency, and a Royal warrant comes down to the Madelonettes, and I was sent about my business with strict injunctions not to show myself again in Paris, under penalty of the Pillory, branding on the cheek with a red-hot iron, and the galleys in perpetuity.

"I had been nearly ten years abroad, and having, by the charity of some Ladies of the Irish Convent in Paris, found means to quit France, landed one morning in the year '90 at Wapping, below London. I had never been in England before, and mighty little I thought of it when I became acquainted with that proud, belly-god country. I found that there was little enough to be done to make a poor Irishwoman able to earn her own living; and that there was besides a prejudice against natives of Ireland, both on account of their Extraction and their Religion, which made the high and mighty English unwilling to employ them, either as day-labourers or as domestic servants. For awhile, getting into loose company, I went about the country to wakes and Fairs, picking up a livelihood by Rope-dancing, back and broadsword fighting, and now and then sword swallowing and fire eating; but since my misadventure with the Posture Master I had taken a dislike to the Mountebank life, and could not settle down to it again. My old love for soldiering revived again, and being at Plymouth where a Recruiting Party was beating up for King William's service in his Irish wars, took a convenient opportunity of quitting my female apparel, resuming that of a man, and listing in Lord Millwood's Regiment of Foot as a private Fusilier. As I knew my drill, and made no secret of my having served in the Maison du Roy, I was looked upon rather as a good prize, for in war time 'tis Soldiers and Soldiers only that are of real value, and they may have served the very Devil himself so that they can trail a pike and cast a grenade: 'tis all one to the Recruiting Captain. He wants men--not loblolly boys--and so long as he gets them he cares not a doit where they come from.

"I suppose I fought as bravely as my neighbours throughout that last Irish Campaign, in which the unhappy King James made so desperate an effort to regain his crown. When King William and the Marshal Duke of Schomberg had made an end of him, and the poor dethroned Monarch had gotten away to St. Germains-en-Laye, there to eke out the remains of his days as a kind of Monk, Millwood's Foot was sent back to England, and put upon the Peace Establishment. That is to say the officers got half pay, and the private men were told that for the next eighteen months they should have sixpence a day, and that after that, unless another war came, they must shift for themselves. I preferred shifting for myself at once to having any of their measly doles after valiant and faithful service; and so, having gathered a very pretty penny out of Plunder while with King William's army, I became a woman again, and opened a Coffee House and Spirit Shop at Chelsea. My curious adventures had by this time come to be pretty well known; and setting up at the sign of the Amazon's Head, with a picture of myself, in full fighting dress splitting an Irish Rapparee with my bayonet, I grew into some renown. The Quality much frequented my house, and some of the book-making gentlemen about Grub Street were good enough to dish up my exploits in a shilling pamphlet, called 'The Life of Elizabeth O----, **alias** James Moriarty, the new Mary Ambree, or the Grenadier.' At Chelsea I remained until the year 1704, but lost much by trusting the Quality, and bad debts among the Gentlemen of the Army. Besides this, I was foolish enough to get married to a worthless, drunken fellow, my own countryman, who had been Fence Master in the Life-Guards, and he very speedily ate me out of House and Home, giving me continual Black Eyes, besides.

"Thus, when the Great War of the Succession broke out, and the English army, commanded by the Great Duke of Marlborough, being allied with the Imperialists under Prince Eugene, and the forces of their High Mightinesses the Dutchmen, went at it Hammer and Tongs about the Spanish succession with King Lewis of France, I, who had always been fond of the army, resolved to give up pot-walloping and take another turn under canvas. It was, however, too late in the day for me to think of again taking the part of a bold Grenadier. I had become somewhat of a Character, and (my old proficiency with the Sticks remaining by me) had earned among the Gentlemen of the Army the cant name of Mother Drum--that by which, to my sorrow, I am now known. And as Mother Drum, suttler and baggage-wagon woman in the train of the great John Churchill, I drank and swore, and sold aquavitae, and plundered when I could, and was flogged when I was taken in the fact (for the Provost-Marshal is no respecter of sex), at Blenheim and Ramilies, and Malplaquet and Oudenarde, and throughout those glorious Campaigns of which I could talk to you till doomsday. I came back to England at the Peace of Utrecht, and set up another Tavern, and married another husband, more worthless and more drunken than the first one, and then went bankrupt and turned washerwoman, and then got into trouble about a gentleman's silver-hilted Rapier, for which I lay long in hold, and was sent for five years to the Plantations; and at last here I am, old and fat and good for nothing, but to throw to the crows as carrion--Mother Drum, God save us all! as bold as brass, and as tough as leather, and 'the miserablest old 'oman that ever stepped.'"

This last part of her adventures I have not polished up, and they are Mother Drum's own.

CHAPTER THE NINTH.

THE END OF MY ADVENTURES AMONG THE BLACKS.

WERE I to give vent to that Garrulity which grows upon us Veterans with Gout and the Gravel, and the kindred Ailments of Age, this Account of my Life would never reach beyond the record of Boyhood. For from the first Flower of my freshest childhood to the time that I became toward the more serious Business of the World, I think I could set down Day by Day, and well-nigh Hour by Hour, all the things that have occurred to me. How is it that I preserve so keen a Remembrance of a little lad's joys and sorrows, when I can scarcely recall how many times I have suffered Shipwreck in later age, or tell how many Sansfoy Miscreants, caring neither for Heaven or man a Point, I have slain? Nay, from what cause does it proceed that I, upon whom the broken reliques of my Schoolmaster's former Cruelty are yet Green, and who can conjure up all the events that bore upon my Running away into Charlwood Chase, even to the doggish names of the Blacks, their ribald talk, and the fleering of the Women they had about them, find it sore travail to remember what I had for dinner yesterday, what friends I conversed with, what Tavern I supped at, what news I read in the Gazette? But 'tis the knowledge of that overweening Craving to count up the trivial Things of my Youth that warns me to use despatch, even if the chronicle of my after doings be but a short summary or sketch of so many Perils by Land and Sea. And for this manner of the remotest things being the more distinct and dilated upon, let me put it to a Man of keen vision, if whirling along a High Road in a rapid carriage, he has not marked, first, that the Palings and Milestones close by have passed beneath him in a confused and jarring swiftness; next, that the Trees, Hedges, &c., of the middle-plan (as the limners call it) have moved slower and with more Deliberation, yet somewhat Fitfully, and encroaching on each other's out-lines; whereas the extreme distance in Clouds, Mountains, far-off Hillsides, and the like, have seemed remote, indeed, but stationary, clear, and unchangeable; so that you could count the fissures in the hoar rocks, and the very sheep still feeding on the smooth slopes, even as they fed fifty years ago? And who (let his later life have been ever so fortunate) does not preferably dwell on that sharp prospect so clearly yet so light looming through the Long Avenue of years?

It was not, I will frankly admit, a very righteous beginning to a young life to be hail-fellow well-met with a Gang of Deerstealers, and to go careering about the King's Forest in quest of Venison which belonged to the Crown. Often have I felt remorseful for so having wronged his Majesty (whom Heaven preserve for the safe-ty of these distraught kingdoms); but what was I, an' it please you, to do? Little Boy Jack was just Little Boy Beggar; and for want of proper Training he became Little Boy Thief. Not that I ever pilfered aught. I was no Candle-snuffer filcher, and, save in the matter of Fat Bucks, the rest of our gang were, indeed, passing honest. Part of the Venison we killed (mostly with a larger kind of Bird-Bolt, or Arbalist Crossbow, for through fear of the keepers we used as little powder and ball as possible) we ate for our Sustenance; for rogues must eat and drink as well as other folks. The greater portion, however, was discreetly conveyed, in carts covered over with garden-stuff, to the market-towns of Uxbridge, Windsor, and Reading, and sold, under the coat-tail as we called it, to Higglers who were in our secret. Sometimes our Merchandise was taken right into London, where we found a good Market with the Fishmongers dwelling about Lincoln's Inn, and who, as they did considerable traffic with the No-bility and Gentry, of whom they took Park Venison, giving them Fish in exchange, were not likely to be suspected of unlawful dealings, or at least were able to make a colourable pretext of Honest Trade to such Constables and Market Conners who had a right to question them about their barterings. From the Fishmongers we took sometimes money and sometimes rich apparel--the cast-off clothes, indeed, of the Nobility, birthday suits or the like, which were not good enough for the Players of Drury Lane and Lincoln's Inn, forsooth, to strut about in on their tragedy-boards, and which they had therefore bestowed upon their domestics to sell. For our Blacks loved to quit their bewrayed apparel at supper-time, and to dress themselves as bravely as when I first tasted their ill-gotten meat at the Stag o' Tyne. From the

Higglers too, we would as willingly take Wine, Strong Waters, and Tobacco, in exchange for our fat and lean, as money; for the Currency of the Realm was then most wofully clipped and defaced, and our Brethren had a wholesome avoidance of meddling with Bank Bills. When, from time to time, one of us ventured to a Market-town, well made-up as a decent Yeoman or Merchant's Rider, 'twas always payment on the Nail and in sounding money for the reckoning. We ran no scores, and paid in no paper.

It was long ere I found out that the Wagon in which I had travelled from the Hercules' Pillars, to be delivered over to Gnawbit, was conducted by one of the most trusted Confederates of our Company; that he took Venison to town for them, and brought them back the Account in specie or needments as they required. And although I am loth to think that the pretty Servant Maid was altogether deceiving me when she told me she was going to see her Grandmother, I fancy that she knew Charlwood Chase, and the gentry that inhabited it, as well as she knew the Pewterer in Panyer Alley. He went a-pewtering no more, if ever he had been 'prentice or done journeywork for that trade, but was neither more nor less than one of the Blacks, and Mistress Slyboots, his Flame, kept him company. Although I hope, I am sure, that they were Married by the Chaplain; for, rough as I am, I had ever a Hatred of Unlawful Passions, and when I am summoned on a Jury, always listen to the King's Proclamation against Vice and Immorality with much gusto and savour.

I stayed with the Blacks in Charlwood Chase until I grew to be a sturdy lad of twelve years of age. I went out with them and followed their naughty courses, and have stricken down many a fat Buck in my time. Ours was the most jovial but the most perilous of lives. The Keepers were always on our track; and sometimes the Sheriff would call out the Posse Comitatis, and he and half the beef-fed tenant-farmers of the country-side would come horsing and hoofing it about the glades to catch us. For weeks together in each year we dared not keep our rendezvous at the Stag, but were fain to hide in Brakes and Hollow Trees, listening to the pursuit as it grew hot and heavy around us; and often with no better Victuals than Pig's-meat and Ditch-water. But then the search would begin to lag; and two or three of the great Squires round about being well terrified by letters written in a liquid designed to counterfeit Blood, with a great Skull and Cross-bones scrawled at the bottom, the whole signed "Captain Night," and telling them that if they dared to meddle with the Blacks their Lives should pay for it, we were left quiet for a season, and could return to our Haunt, there to feast and carouse according to custom. Nor am I slow to believe that some of the tolerance we met with was due to our being known to the County Gentry as stanch Tories, and as stanch detesters of the House of Hanover (I speak, of course, of my companions, for I was of years too tender to have any politics). We never killed a Deer but on the nearest tree some one of us out with his Jack-knife and carved on the bark of it, "Slain by King James's order;" or, if there were no time for so long a legend, or the Beast was stricken in the Open, a simple K. J. (which the Hanover Rats understood well enough, whether cut in the trunk or the turf) sufficed. The Country Gentlemen were then of a very furious way of thinking concerning the rights of the present Illustrious House to the Throne; but Times do alter, and so likewise do Men's Thoughts and Opinions, and I dare swear there is no Brunswicker or Church of England man more leal at this present writing than John Dangerous.

Captain Night, to whom I was a kind of Page or Henchman, used me with much tenderness. Whenever at supper the tongues grew too loosened, and wild talk, and of the wickedese, began to jingle among the bottles and glasses, he would bid me Withdraw, and go keep company for a time with Mistress Slyboots. Captain Night was a man of parts and even of letters; and I often wondered why he, who seemed so well fitted to Shine even among the Great, should pass his time among Rogues, and take the thing that was not his. He was often absent from us for many days, sometimes for nigh a month; and would return sunburnt and travel-stained, as though he had been journeying in Foreign Parts. He was always very thoughtful and reserved after these Gaddings about; and Mistress Slyboots, the Maid, used to say that he was in Love, and had been playing the gallant to some fine Madam. But I thought otherwise: for at this season it was his custom to bring back a Valise full to the very brim of letters and papers, the which he would take Days to read and re-read, noting and seemingly copying some, but burning the greater portion. At this season he would refrain from joining the Gang, and honourably forswore his share of their plunder, always giving Mother Drum a broad piece for each night's Supper, Bottle, and Bed. But when his pressing business was over, no man was keener in the chase, or brought down the quarry so skilfully as Captain Night. He loved to have me with him, to talk to and Question me; and it was one day, after I had told him that the Initial letter D was the only clue to my Grandmother's name, which I had seen graven on her Coffin-plate, he must needs tell me that if she were Madam (or rather Lady) D----, I must needs, as a Kinsman, be D---- too, and that he would piece out the name, and call me Dangerous. So that I was Little Boy Jack no more, and John Dangerous I have been from that day to this. Not but what my Ancestry and Belongings might warrant me in assuming another title, than which--so far as lineage counts--Bourbon or Nassau could not rank much higher. But the name of Dangerous has pleased me alway; it has stood me in stead in many a hard pass, and I am content to abide by it now that my locks are gray, and the walls of this my battered old tenement are crumbling into decay.

'Twas I alone that was privileged to stay with Captain Night when he was doing Secretary's work among his papers; for, save when Mistress Slyboots came up to him--discreetly tapping at the door first, you may be sure--with a cup of ale and a toast, he would abide no other company. And on such days I wore not my Black Disguisement, but the better clothes he had provided for me,--a little Riding Suit of red drugget, silver-laced, and a cock to my hat like a Military Officer,--and felt myself as grand as you please. I never dared speak to him until he spoke to me; but used to sit quietly enough sharpening bolts or twisting bowstrings, or cleaning his Pistols, or furbishing up his Hanger and Belt, or suchlike boyish pastime-labour. He was careful to burn every paper that he Discarded after taking it from the Valise; but once, and once only, a scrap remained unconsumed on the hearth, the which, with my ape-like curiosity of half-a-score summers, I must needs spell over, although I got small good therefrom. 'Twas but the top of a letter, and all the writing I could make out ran,

"St. Germains, August the twelfth.
"MY DEAR" ...
and here it broke off, and baffled me.

Whenever Captain Night went a hunting, I attended upon him; but when he was away, I was confided to the care of Jowler, who, albeit much given to babble in his liquor, was about the most discreet (the Chaplain always excepted) among the Gang. In the dead season, when Venison was not to be had, or was nothing worth for the Market if it had been killed, we lived mostly on dried meats and cured salmon; the first prepared by Mother Drum and her maid, the last furnished us by our good friends and Chapmen the Fishmongers about Lincoln's Inn. And during this same Dead Season, I am glad to say that my Master did not suffer me to remain idle; but, besides taking some pains in tutoring me himself, moved our Chaplain, all of whose humane letters had not been washed out by burnt Brandy or fumed out by Tobacco (to the use of which he was immoderately given), to put me through a course of daily instruction. I had had some Latin beaten into me by Gnawbit, when he had nothing of more moment to bestir himself about, and had attained a decent proficiency in reading and writing. Under the Chaplain of the Blacks, who swore at me grievously, but never, under the direst forbidding, laid finger on me, I became a current scholar enough of my own tongue, with just such a little smattering of the Latin as helped me at a pinch in some of the Secret Dealings of my later career. But Salt Water has done its work upon my Lily's Grammar; and although I yield to no man in the Faculty of saying what I mean, ay, and of writing it down in good plain English ('tis true that of your nominatives and genitives and stuff, I know nothing), I question if I could tell you the Latin for a pair of riding-boots.

There was a paltry parcel of books at the Stag o' Tyne, and these I read over and over again at my leisure. There was a History of the Persecutions undergone by the Quakers, and Bishop Sprat's Narrative of the Conspiracy of Blackhead and the others against him. There was Foxe's Martyrs, and God's Revenge against Murder (a very grim tome), and Mr. Daniel Defoe's Life of Moll Flanders, and Colonel Jack. These, with two or three Play-books, and a Novel of Mrs. Aphra Behn (very scurrilous), a few Ballads, and some ridiculous Chap-books about Knights and Fairies and Dragons, made up the tattered and torn library of our house in Charlwood Chase. 'Twas good enough, you may say, for a nest of Deerstealers. Well, there might have been a worse one; but these, I can aver, with English and Foreign newspapers and letters, and my Bible in later life, have been all the reading that John Dangerous can boast of. Which makes me so mad against your fine Scholars and Scribblers, who, because they can turn verse and make Te-to-tum into Greek, must needs sneer at me at the Coffee House, and make a butt of an honest man who has been from one end of the world to the other, and has fought his way through it to Fortune and Honour.

I was in the twelfth year of my age, when a great change overtook me in my career. Moved, as it would seem, to exceeding Anger and implacable Disgust by the carryings-on of Captain Night and his merry men in Charlwood Chase, the King's Ministers put forth a Proclamation against us, promising heavy Blood Money to any who would deliver us, or any one member of the Gang, into the hands of Authority. This Proclamation came at first to little. There was no sending a troop of horse into the Chase, and the husbandmen of the country-side were too good Friends of ours to play the Judas. We were not Highway Robbers. Not one of our band had ever taken to or been taken from the Road. Rascals of the Cartouche and Macheath kidney we Disdained. We were neither Foot-pads nor Cut-purses, nay, nor Smugglers nor Rick-burners. We were only Unfortunate Gentlemen, who much did need, and who had suffered much for our politics and our religion, and had no other means of earning a livelihood than by killing the King's Deer. Those peasants whom we came across Feared us, indeed, as they would the very Fiend, but bore us no malice; for we always treated them with civility, and not rarely gave them the Umbles and other inferior parts of the Deer, against their poor Christenings and Lyings-in. And through these means, and some small money presents our Captain would make to their wives and callow brats, it came to pass that Mother Drum had seldom cause to brew aught but the smallest beer, for morning Drinking; for though we had to pay for our Wine and Ardent Drinks, the cellar of the Stag o' Tyne was always handsomely furnished with barrels of strong ale, which Lobbin Clout or Colin Mayfly, the Hind or the Plough-churl, would bring us secretly by night in their Wains for gratitude. I know not where they got the malt from, but there was narrow a fault to find with the Brew. I recollect its savour now with a sweet tooth, condemned as I am to the inky Hog's-wash which the Londoners call Porter; and indeed it is fit for Porters to drink, but not for Gentlemen. These Peasants used to tremble all over with terror when they came to the Stag o' Tyne; but they were always hospitably made welcome, and sent away with full gizzards, ay, and with full heads too, and by potions to which the louts were but little used.

We had no fear of treachery from these Chawbacons, but we had Enemies in the Chase nevertheless. Here dwelt a vagabond tribe of Bastard Verderers and Charcoal-burners, savage, ignorant, brutish Wretches, as superstitious as the Manilla Creoles. They were one-half gipsies, and one half, or perhaps a quarter, trade-fallen whippers-in and keepers that had been stripped of their livery. They picked up their sorry crust by burning of charcoal, and carting of dead wood to farmers for to consume in their ingles. Now and again, when any of the Quality came to hunt in the Chase, the Head Keeper would make use of a score or so of them as beaters and rabble-prickers of the game; but nine months out of the twelve they rather starved than lived. These Charcoal-burners hated us Blacks, first, because in our sable disguise we rather imitated their own Beastly appearance--for the varlets never washed from Candlemas to Shrovetide; next, because we were Gentlemen; and lastly, because we would not suffer them to catch Deer for themselves in pit-falls and springes. Nay, a True Gentleman Black meeting a "Coaley," as we called the charcoal fellows, with so much as a hare, a rabbit, or a pheasant with him, let alone venison, would ofttimes give him a sackful of sore bones to carry as well as a game-bag. No "Coaley" was ever let to slake his thirst at the Stag o' Tyne. The poor wretches had a miserable hovel of an inn to their own part on the western outskirts of the Chase, a place by the sign of the Hand and Hatchet, where they ate their rye-bread and drank their sour Clink, when they could muster coppers enough for a twopenny carouse.

This Proclamation, of which at first we made light, was speedily followed by a real live Act of Parliament, which is yet, I have been told, Law, and is known as the "Black Act."[M] The most dreadful punishments were denounced against us by the Houses of Lords and Commons, and the Blood Money was doubled. One of the most noted Thief-takers of that day--almost as great a one as Jonathan Wild--comes down post, and sets up his Standard at Reading, as though he had been King William on the banks of the Boyne. With him he brings a mangy Rout of Constables and Bailiff's Followers, and other kennel-ranging vagabonds; and now nothing must serve him but to beg of the Commanding Officer at Windsor (my Lord Treherne) for a loan of two companies of the Foot Guards, who, nothing loth for field-sport and extra pay, were placed, with their captain and all--more shame for a Gentle-man to mix in such Hangman's work!--under Mr. Thief-taker's orders. He and his Bandogs, ay, and his Grenadiers, might have hunted us through Charlwood Chase until Doomsday but for the treachery of the "Coaleys." 'Twas one of their number,--named, or rather nicknamed, "the Beau," because he washed his face on Sunday, and was therefore held to be of the first fashion,--who earned eighty pounds by revealing the hour when the whole Gang of Blacks might be pounced upon at the

Stag o' Tyne. The infamous wretch goes to Aylesbury,--for our part of the Chase was in the county of Bucks,--and my Thief-taking gentleman from Reading meets him--a pretty couple; and he makes oath before Mr. Justice Cribfee (who should have set him in the Stocks, or delivered him over to the Beadle for a vagrant); and after a fine to-do of Sheriff's business and swearing in of special constables, the end of it was, that a whole Rout of them, Sheriff, Javelin-men, and Headboroughs and all, with the Grenadiers at their back, came upon us unawares one moonlight night as we were merrily supping at the Stag.

'Twas no use showing Fight perhaps, for we were undermanned, some of us being away on the scent, for we suspected some foul play. The constables and other clod-hopping Alguazils were all armed to the teeth with Bills and Blunderbusses, Pistols and Hangers; but had they worn all the weapons in the Horse Armoury in the Tower, it would not have saved them from shivering in their shoes when "Hard and sharp" was the word, and an encounter with the terrible Blacks had to be endured. We should have made mince-meat of them all, and perhaps hanged up one or two of them outside the inn as an extra signpost. But we were not only unarmed, we were overmatched, my hearties. There were the Redcoats, burn them! How many times in my life have I been foiled and baffled by those miscreated men-machines in scarlet blanketing! No use in a stout Heart, no use in a strong Hand, no use in a sharp Sword, or a pair of barkers with teeth that never fail, when you have to do with a Soldier. Do! What are you to do with him? There he is, with his shaven face and his hair powdered, as if he were going to a fourpenny fandango at Bagnigge Wells. There he is, as obstinate as a Pig, and as firm as a Rock, with his confounded bright firelock, bayonet, and crossbelts. There he is, immoveable and unconquerable, defying the boldest of Smugglers, the bravest of Gentlemen Rovers, and, by the Lord Harry, *he eats you up*. Always give the Redcoats a wide berth, my dear, and the Grenadiers more than all.

Unequal as were the odds, with all these Roaring Dragons in scarlet baize on our trail, we had still a most desperate fight for it. While the mob of Constables kept cowering in the bar-room down-stairs, crying out to us to surrender in the King's name,--I believe that one poor creature, the Justice of Peace, after getting himself well walled up in a corner with chairs and tables, began to quaver out the King's Proclamation against the Blacks,--the plaguy Soldiers came blundering up both pair of stairs, and fell upon us Billy Boys tooth and nail. 'Slid! my blood simmers when I think of it. Over went the tables and settles! Smash went trenchers and cups and glasses! Clink-a-clink went sword-blades and bayonets! "And don't fire, my lads!" cries out the Soldier-officer to his Grannies. "We want all these rogues to hang up at Aylesbury Gaol."

"Rogue yourself, and back to your Mother!" cries Captain Night, very pale; but I never saw him look Bolder or Handsomer. "Rogue in your Tripes, you Hanover Rat!" and he shortens his sword and rushes on the Soldier-officer.

The Grenadier Captain was brave enough, but he was but a smockfaced lad fresh from the Mall and St. James's Guard-room, and he had no chance against a steady practised Swordsman and Forest Blood, as Captain Night was. We all thought he would make short work of the Soldier-officer. He had him in a corner, and the Chaplain, a-top of whom was a Grenadier trying to throttle or capture him, or both, exclaims, "Give him the grace-blow, my dear; give it him under the fifth rib!" when Captain Night cries, "Go home to your mother, Milksop!" and he catches his own sword by the hilt, hits his Enemy a blow on the right wrist enough to numb it for a month, twists his fingers in his cravat, flings him on one side, and right into the middle of a punch-bowl, and then, upon my word, he himself jumps out of Window, shouting out, "Follow me, little Jack Dangerous!"

I wished for nothing better, and had already my leg on the sill, when two great hulking Grenadiers seized hold of me. 'Twas then, for the first time, that I earned a just claim and title to the name of Dangerous; for a little dirk I was armed with being wrested from me by Soldier number one, who eggs on his comrade to collar the young Fox-cub, as he calls me, I seize a heavy Stone Demijohn fall of brandy, and smash it goes on the head of Soldier number two. He falls with a dismal groan, the blood and brandy running in equal measure from his head, and the first Soldier runs his bayonet through me.

Luckily, 'twas but a flesh-wound in the flank, and no vital part was touched. It was enough for me, however, poor Urchin,--enough to make me tumble down in a dead faint; and when I came to myself, I found that I had been removed to the bar-room down-stairs, where I made one of nineteen Blacks, all prisoners to the King for stealing his Deer, and all bound hand and foot with Ropes.

"Never mind their hurting your wrists, young Hempseed," chuckled one of the scaldpated constable rogues who was guarding us. "You'll have enough to tighten your gullet after 'Sizes, as sure as eggs is eggs."

"Nay, brother Grimstock, the elf's too young to be hanged," puts in another constable, with somewhat of a charitable visage.

"Too young!" echoes he addressed as Grimstock. "'Twas bred in the bone in him, the varmint, and the Gallows Fever will come out in the flesh. Too young! he was weaned on rue, and rode between his Father's legs (that swung) i' the cart to Tyburn, and never sailed a cockboat but in Execution Dock. My tobacco-box to a tester an' he dance not on nothing if he comes to holding up his hand before Judge Blackcap, that never spared but one in the Calendar, and then 'twas by Mistake."

These were not very comfortable news for me, poor manacled wretch; and with a great bayonet-wound in my side to boot, that had been but clumsily dressed by a village Leech, who was, I suspect, a Farrier and Cow Doctor as well. But I have always found, in this life's whirligig, that when your Case is at the worst (unless a Man indeed Dies, when there is nothing more to be done), it is pretty sure to mend, if you lie quiet and let things take their chance. I could not be much worse off than I was, wounded and friendless, and a captive; and so I held my tongue, and let them use me as they would. Some scant comfort was it, however, to find, when the battle-field was gone over, that, besides the Grenadier whose crown I had cracked, another had been pistolled by Jowler, and and lay mortally wounded, and Groaning Dismally. Poor Jowler himself would never pistol Foe more. He was dead; for the Men of War, furious at our desperate Resistance, at the worsting of their fine-feathered officer (who was mumbling of his bruised hand as a down-trodden Hound would its paw, and cursing meanwhile, which Dogs use not to do), and driven to Mad Rage by the escape of Captain Night, had fired pell-mell into a Group of which Jowler made one, and so killed him. A bullet through his brain set him clean quit of all indictments under the Black Act, before our Sovereign Lord the King. Likewise was it a matter of rejoicing for our party that, after long seeking the Traitor Coaley, the wretched "Beau" was found duly strangled, and completely a corpse on the staircase. There was something curious about the manner of justice coming to this villain. The Deed had been done with no weapon more Lethal than an old Stocking; yet so tightly was it tied round his false neck, that it had to be cut off piecemeal, and even then the ribs of the worsted were found to be Imbedded, and to have made Furrows in his flesh. Now it is certain that we Blacks had not laid about us with old Wives' hose, any more than we had lunged at our enemies with knitting-needles. There, however, was Monsieur Judas, as dead as a Dolphin two hours on deck. Lord, what an ugly countenance had the losel when they came to wash the charcoal off him! As to who had forestalled the Hangman in his office, no certain testimony could be given. I have always found at Sea, when any doubts arise as to the why and the wherefore of a gentleman's death, that the best way to settle accounts is to fling him overboard; but on dry land your plaguy Dead Body is a sore Stumbling Block, and Impediment, always turning up when it is not Wanted, and bringing other Gentlemen into all kinds of trouble. Crowner's Quest was held on the "Beau;" and I only wonder that they did not bring it in murder against Me. The jury sat a long time without making up their minds, till the Parish constable ordered them in a bowl of Flip, upon which they proceeded to bring in a verdict of Wilful Murder against some person or persons unknown. I can scarcely, to this day, bring myself to suspect my pretty maid, that should have married the Pewterer, of such a bold Act, and the rather believe that it was the girl Grip and her Mistress that worked off the Spy and Traitor between them. Not that Mother Drum would have needed any assistance in the mere doing of the thing. She was a Mutton-fisted woman, and as strong in the forearm as a Bridewell correctioner.

Oh, the dreary journey we made that morning to Aylesbury! The Men Blacks were tied back to back, and thrown into such carts as could be pressed into the service from the farmsteads on the skirts of the Chase. One of the constables must needs offer, the Scoundrel, to take horse and go borrow a cartload of fetters from the gaoler at Reading; but he was overruled, and Ropes were thought strong enough to confine us. There was no chance, alas! of any rescue; for those of our comrades who had been fortunate enough through absence to avoid capture, had doubtless by this time scent of the Soldiers, and there was no kicking against those bright Firelocks and Bayonets. Yet had there been another escape. Cicely Grip and Mother Drum were taken, but the pretty maid I loved so for her kindness to me when I was Forlorn had shown a clean pair of heels, and was nowhere to be found. Good luck to her, I thought. Perchance she has met with Captain Night, and they are Safe and Sound by this time, and off to Foreign Parts. For in all this I declare I saw nothing Wrong, and held, in my baby logic, that we Blacks had all been very harshly entreated by the Constables and Redcoats, and that it was a shame to use us so. Mother Drum, the Wench, and my poor wounded Self, were put into one cart together, and through Humanity, a Sergeant (for the Constables would not have done it) bade his men litter down some straw for us to lie upon. There was a ragged Tilt too over the cart; and thinks I, in a Gruesome manner, "The first time you rode on straw under a Tilt, Jack, you were going to school, and now, 'ifegs, you are going to be Hanged." For it was settled on all sides, and even he with the Charitable Countenance came to be of that mind at last, that my fate was to die by the Cord.

"Why," says one, "you've half-brained Corporal Foss with the Demijohn; never did liquor get into a pretty man's head so soon and so deep. They'll stretch your neck for this, my poult,--they will."

The Sergeant interposing, said that perhaps, if interest were made for me, I might be spared an Indictment, and let to go and serve the King as a Drummer till I was old enough to carry a firelock. But at this the soldiers shook their heads; for Captain Poppingjay, their officer, was, it seems, still in a towering rage at having had his fine-lady's hand so wofully mauled by Captain Night, and vowed vengeance against the whole crew of poachers and their whelp, as he must needs be Polite enough to call me.

This Fine Gentleman had been provided with a Horse by the Sheriff, and, as he rode by the cart where I and Drum and the Girl were jogging on, he spies me under the Tilt, and in his cruel manner makes a cut at me with his riding wand, calling me a young spawn of Thievery and Rebellion.

"You coward," I cried in a passion; "you daren't a' done that if my hands were loose, and I hadn't this baggonet-wound in me."

"Shame to hit the boy," growled the charitable Constable, who was on horse-back too.

The Soldier-officer turned round quickly to see who had spoken; but the Sergeant, who watched him, pointed with his halbert to the Constable, and he returned the Captain's glance with a sturdy mien. So my Fine Gentleman reins in his beast and lets us pass, eyeing his hand, which was all wrapped up in Bandages, and muttering that it was well none of his own fellows had given him this sauciness.

The day was a dreadful one. How many times our train halted to bait I know not; but this I know, that I fainted often from Agony of my wound and the uneasy motion of my carriage. It is a wonder that I ever came to my journey's end alive, and in all likelihood never should, but for the unceasing care and solicitude of the two poor women who were with me, Prisoners like myself, but full of merciful kindness for one who was in a sorer strait than they. By earnest pleading did Mother Drum persuade the Head Constable--who, the nearer we got to gaol the more authority he took, and the less he seemed to think of our soldier escort--to allow her hands to be unbound that she might minister unto me; and also did she obtain so much grace as for some of the Money belonging unto her, and which had been seized at the Stag o' Tyne, to be spent in buying of a bottle of brandy at one of our halting-places, with which she not only comforted herself and her afflicted Maid, but, mingling it with water, cooled my parched tongue and bathed my forehead.

Brandy was the only medicament this good soul knew; and more lives she averred, had been saved by Right Nantz than lost by bad B. W.; but still brandy was not precisely the kind of physic to give a Patient who before Sundown was in a Raging Fever. But 'twas all one to the Law; and coming at last to my journey's end, we were all, the wounded and the whole, flung into Gaol to answer for it at the 'Sizes.

NOTE:
[M] See the Statutes at Large. The Black Act was repealed mainly through the exertions of Sir James Macintosh, early in the present century. Under its clauses the going about "disguised or blackened in pursuit of game" was made felony without benefit of clergy; the punishment thereof death.--ED.

CHAPTER THE TENTH.

I AM VERY NEAR BEING HANGED.

OUR prison was surely the most loathsome hole that Human beings were ever immured in. It was a Horrible and Shameful Place, conspicuous for such even in those days, when every prison was a place of Horror and Shame. 'Twas one of the King's Prisons,--one of His Majesty's Gaols,-- the county had nothing to do with it; and the Keeper thereof was a Woman. Say a Tigress rather; but Mrs. Macphilader wore a hoop and lappets and gold ear-rings, and was dubbed "Madam" by her Underlings. Here you might at any time have seen poor Wretches chained to the floor of reeking dungeons, their arms, legs, necks even, laden with irons, themselves abused, beaten, jeered at, drenched with pailfuls of foul water, and more than three-quarter starved, merely for not being able to pay Garnish to the Gaoleress, or comply with other her exorbitant demands. Fetters, indeed, were common and Fashionable Wear in the Gaol. 'Twas pleaded that the walls of the prison were so rotten through age, and the means of guarding the prisoners--for they could not be always calling in the Grenadiers--so limited, that they must needs put the poor creatures in the bilboes, or run the chance of their escaping every day in the week. Thus it came to pass, even, that they were tried in Fetters, and sometimes could not hold up their hands (weakened besides by the Gaol Distemper), at the bidding of the Clerk of the Arraigns, for the weight of the Manacles that were upon them. And it is to the famous and admirable Mr. John Howard that we owe the putting down of this last Abomination.

We lay so long in this dreadful place before a Gaol Delivery was made, that my wound, bad as it was, had ample time to heal, leaving only a great indented cicatrix, as though some Giant had forced his finger into my flesh, and of which I shall never be rid. Two more of our gang died of the Gaol Fever before Assize time; one was so fortunate as to break prison, file the irons off his legs, and get clear away; and another (who was always of a Melancholy turn) hanged himself one morning, in a halter made from strips of his blanket knotted together. The rest of us were knocked about by the Turnkeys, or abused by the Gaoleress, Mrs. Macphilader, pretty much as they liked. We were, however, not so badly off as some of the poor prisoners--sheep-stealers, footpads, vagrom men and women, and the like, or even as some of the poor Debtors--many of whom lay here incarcerate years after they had discharged the Demands of their Creditors against them, and only because they could not pay their Fees. We Blacks were always well supplied with money; and money could purchase almost any thing in a prison in those days. Roast meats, and wine and beer and punch, pipes and tobacco, and playing cards and song-books,-- all these were to be had by Gentlemen Prisoners; the Gaoleress taking a heavy toll, and making a mighty profit from all these luxurious things. But there was one thing that money could not buy, namely, cleanly lodging; for the State Room, a hole of a place, very meanly furnished, where your great Smugglers or ruffling Highwaymen were sometimes lodged, at a guinea a day for their accommodation, was only so much better from the common room in so far as the prisoner had bed and board to himself; but for nastiness and creeping things--which I wonder, so numerous were they, did not crawl away with the whole prison bodily: but 'tis hard to find those that are unanimous, even vermin.--For all that made the Gaol most thoroughly hateful and dreadful, there was not a pin to choose between the State Room, the Common Side, and the Rat's Larder, Clink, or Dark Dungeon, where the Poor were confined in wantonness, and the Stubborn were kept sometimes for punishment; for Madam Gaoleress had a will of her own, and would brook no incivilities from her Lodgers; so sure is it, that falling out one day on the disputed Question of a bottle of Aquavitae on which toll had not been paid, she calls one of the Turnkeys and bids him clap Mother Drum into the Stocks (that stood in the Prison Yard) for an hour or two, for the cooling of her temper. But this had just the contrary effect; for the whilom Hostess of the Stag o' Tyne, enraged at the Indignity offered to her, did so bemaul and bewray Madam Macphilader with her tongue, shaking her fist at her meanwhile, that the Gaoleress in a fury clawed at least two handfuls of M. Drum's hair from her head, not without getting some smart clapperclawing in the face; whereupon she cries out "Murther" and "Mutiny" and "Prisonrupt," and sends post-haste for Justice Palmworm, her gossip indeed, and one of those trading magistrates that so disgraced our bench before Mr. Henry Fielding the writer stirred up Authority to put some order therein. The Justice comes; and he and the Gaoleress, after cracking a bottle of mulled port between them, poor Mother Drum was brought up before his Worship for mutinous conduct. The Justice would willingly have compounded the case, for Lucre was his only love; but 'twas vengeance the Gaoleress hankered after; and the end of it was that poor Mother Drum was triced up at the post that was by the Stocks, and had a dozen and a half from a cat with indeed but three tails, but that, I warrant, hurt pretty nigh as sharply as nine would have done in weaker hands; for 'twas the Gaoleress that played the Beadle and laid on the Scourge.

At length, when I was quite tired out, and, knowing nothing of the course of Law, began to think that we were doomed to perpetual Imprisonment, His Majesty's Judges of Assize came upon their circuit, and those whom the Fever and Want and the Duresse of their Keeper had spared were put upon their trial. By this time I was thought well enough, though as gaunt as a Hound, to be put in the same Gaol-bird's trim as my companions; so a pair of Woman's fetters--ay, my friends, the women wore fetters in those days--were put upon me; and the whole of us, all shackled as we were, found ourselves, one fine Monday morning, in the Dock, having been driven thereinto very much after the fashion of a flock of sheep. The Court was crowded, for the case against the Blacks had made a prodigious stir; and the King's Attorney, the most furious Person for talking a Fellow-creature's Life away that ever I remember to have seen or heard, came down especially from London to prosecute us. Neither he nor His Lordship the Judge, in his charge to the Grand Jury, had any but the worst of words to give us; and folks began to say that this would be another Bloody Assize; that the Shire Hall had need to be hung with scarlet, as when Jeffreys was on the bench; and that as short work would be made of us as of the Rebels in the West. And I did not much care, for I was sick of lying in hold, amidst Evil Odours, and with a green wound. It came even to whispering that one of us at least would be made a Gibbeting-in-chains example for killing the Grenadier, if that Act could be fixed on any particular Black. And half in jest, half in earnest, the Woman-Keeper told me on the morning of the Assizes that, young as I was (not yet twelve years of age), my bones might rattle in a birdcage in the midst of Charlwood Chase; for if I could brain one Grenadier, I could kill another. But yet, being so weary of the Life, I did not much Care.

It was still somewhat of a Relief to me to come into the Dock, and look upon State and Rich Clothes (in which I have always taken a Gentleman-like pleasure), in the stead of all the dirt and squalor which for so long had been my surrounding. There were the Judges all ranged, a Terrible show, in their brave Scarlet Robes and Fur Tippets, with great monstrous Wigs, and the King's Arms behind them under a Canopy, done in Carver's work, gilt. They frowned on us dreadfully when we came trooping into the Dock, bringing all manner of Deadly pestilential Fumes with us from the Gaol yonder, and which not all the rue, rosemary, and marjoram strewn on the Dock-ledge, nor the hot vinegar sprinkled about the Court, could mitigate. The middle Judge, who was old, and had a split lip and a fang protruding from it, shook his head at me, and put on such an Awful face, that for a moment my scared thoughts went back to the Clergyman at St. George's, Hanover Square, that was wont to be so angry with me in his Sermons. Ah, how different was the lamentable Hole in the which I now found myself cheek by jowl with Felons and Caravats, to the great red-baize Pew in which I had sat so often a Little Gentleman! He to the right of the middle Judge was a very sleepy gentleman, and scarcely ever woke up during the proceedings, save once towards one of the clock, when he turned to his Lordship (whom I had at once set down as Mr. Justice Blackcap, and was in truth that Dread Functionary), saying, "Brother, is it dinner-time?" But his Lordship to the left, who had an old white face like a sheep, and his wig all awry, was of a more placable demeanour, and looked at me, poor luckless Outcast, with some interest. I saw him turn his head and whisper to the gentleman they told me was the High Sheriff, and who sat on the Bench alongside the Judges, very fine, in a robe and gold chain, and with a great sheathed sword behind him, resting on a silver goblet. Then the High Sheriff took to reading over the Calendar, and shrugged his shoulders, whereupon I indulged in some Hope. Then he leans over to Mr. Clerk of the Arraigns, pointing me out, and seemingly asking him some question about me; but that gentleman hands him up a couple of parchments, and my quick Ear (for the Court was but small) caught the words, "There are two Indictments against him, Sir John." Whereupon they looked at me no more, save with a Stern and Sorrowful

Gravity; and the Hope I had nourished for a moment departed from me. Yet then, as afterwards, and as now, I found (although then too babyish to reason about it), that, bad as we say the World is, it is difficult to come upon Three Men together in it but that one is Good and Merciful.

I feel that my disclaimer notwithstanding the Bark of my Narrative is running down the stream of a Garrulous talkativeness; but I shall be more brief anon. And what would you have? If there be any circumstances which should entitle a man to give chapter and verse, they must surely be those under which he was Tried for his Life.

The first day we only held up our hands, and heard the Indictment against us read. Some of us who were Moneyed had retained Counsellors from London to cross-question the witnesses; for to speak to the Jury in aid of Prisoners, who could not often speak for themselves, the Gentlemen of the Law were not then permitted. And this I have ever held to be a crying Injustice. There was no one, however, not so much as a Pettifogger, to lift tongue, or pen, or finger, to save little Jack Dangerous from the Rope. My Protector, Captain Night, was at large; Jowler, my first friend among the Blacks, was dead; and, as Misery is apt to make men Selfish, the rest of my companions had entirely forgotten how friendless and deserted I was. But, just as we were going back to Gaol, up comes to the spikes of the Dock a gentleman with a red face, and a vast bushy powdered wig, like a cauliflower in curls. He wore a silk cassock and sash, and was the Ordinary; but he had forgotten, I think, to come into the Prison and read prayers to us. He kept those ministrations against such time as the Cart was ready, and the Tree decked with its hempen garland. This gentlemen beckons me, and asks if I have any Counsellor. I told him, No; and that I had no Friends ayont Mother Drum, and she was laid up, sick of a pair of sore shoulders. He goes back to the Bench and confers with the Gentlemen, and by and by the Clerk of the Arraigns calls out that, through the Humanity of the Sheriff, the prisoner John Dangerous was to have Counsel Assigned to him. But it would have been more Humane, I think, to have let the Court and the World know that I was a poor neglected Castaway, knowing scarcely my right Hand from my left, and that all I had done had been in that Blindfoldedness of Ignorance which can scarcely, I trust, be called Sin.

Back, however, we went to Gaol, and a great Rout there was made that night by Mrs. Macphilader for the payment of all arrears of Fees and Garnish to her; for, you see, being a prudent Woman, she feared lest some of the prisoners should be Acquitted, or Discharged on proclamation. And our Gang of Blacks, for whose aid their friends in ambush--and they had friends in all kinds of holes and corners, as I afterwards discovered to my surprise--had mostly bountifully come forward, did not trouble themselves much about the peril they were in, but bestowed themselves of making a Roaring Night. And hindered by none in Authority,--for the Gaolers and Turnkeys in those days were not above drinking, and smoking, and singing, and dicing with their charges,--they did keep it up so merrily and so roaringly, that the best part of the night was spent before drowsiness came over Aylesbury Gaol.

Then the next day to Court, and there the Judges as before, and Sir John the High Sheriff, and the Counsel for the Crown and for us, and twelve honest gentlemen in a box by themselves, that were of the Petty Jury, to try us; and, I am ashamed to say, a great store of Ladies, all in ribbons and patches and laces and fine clothes, that sate some on the Bench beside the Judges, and others in the body of the Court among the Counsel, and stared at us miserable objects in the Dock as though we had been a Galantee Show. It is some years now since I have entered a Court of Criminal Justice, and I do hope that this Indecent and Uncivil Behaviour of well-bred Women coming to gaze on Criminals for their diversion has utterly given way before the Benevolence and good taste of a polite Age.

When, at the last, I was told to plead, and at the bidding of an Officer of the Court, who stood underneath me, had pleaded Not Guilty, and had been asked how I would be tried, and had answered, likewise at his bidding, "By God and my Country," and when after that the Clerk of the Arraigns had prayed Heaven--and I am sure I needed it, and thanked him heartily at the time, kind Gentleman, thinking that he meant it, and not knowing that it was a mere Legal Form--to send me a good Deliverance,--the Judge bids me, to my great surprise, to Stand By. I thought at first that they were going to have Mercy on me, and would have down on my knees in gratitude to them. But it was not so; and the sleepy old Judge, suddenly waking up, told me that there were two Indictments against me, and that I should have the honour of being tried separately. Goodness save us! I was looked upon as one of the most desperate of the Gang, and was to be tried, not only under the Black Act, but that, not having the fear of God before my eyes, but being moved by the instigation of the Devil, I had, against the peace of our Sovereign Lord the King, attempted feloniously to kill, slay, and murder one John Foss, a Corporal in his Majesty's Regiment of Grenadier Footguards, by striking him, the said John Foss, over the back, breast, hips, loins, shoulders, thighs, legs, feet, arms, and fingers, with a certain deadly and lethal weapon, to wit, with a demijohn of Brandy.

I was put back and kept all day in the prison. At evening came in my comrades, and from them I learnt that the case had gone dead against them from the beginning, that the Jury had found them guilty under the Statute without leaving the box; and that, as the felony was one without the benefit of Clergy, Judge Blackcap had put on a wig as black as his name, and sentenced every man Jack of them to be hanged on the Monday week next following.

So then it came to my turn to be tried. The ordeal on the first Indictment was very short; for, at the Judge's bidding, the Jury acquitted me of trying to murder Corporal Foss before I had been ten minutes in the dock. I did not understand the proceedings in the least at that time; but I was told afterwards that the clever legal gentleman who had drawn up the Indictment against me, while very particularly setting down the parts of the body on which I might have struck Corporal Foss, omitted to specify the one place, namely, his head, on which I did hit him. Counsel for the Crown endeavoured, indeed, to prove that a splinter from the broken demijohn had grazed the corporal's finger, but the evidence for this fell dead. And, again, it coming out that I was arraigned as John Danger, whereas I had given the name of John Dangerous, to which I had perhaps no more right than to that of the Pope of Rome, the Judge roundly tells the Jury that the Indictment is bad in law, and I was forthwith acquitted as aforesaid.

But I was not scot-free. There was that other Indictment under the Black Act; and in that, alas, there was no flaw. The Solemn Court freed itself, to be sure, of the Mockery of finding a child under twelve years Guilty of the attempted murder of a Grenadier six feet high; but no less did the witnesses swear, and the Judge sum up, and Counsel for the Crown insist, and my Counsel feebly deny, and the Jury at last fatally find against me, that I had gone about armed and Disguised by night, and wandered up and down in the King's Forests, and stolen his Deer, and Goodness can tell what besides; and so, being found guilty, the middle Judge puts on his black cap again, and tells me that I am to be hanged on Monday week by the neck.

He did not say any thing about my youth, or about my utter loneliness, or about the evil examples which had brought me to this Pass. Perhaps it was not his Duty, but that of the Ordinary, to tell me so. The Hanging was his department, the praying belonged to his Reverence. They led me back to prison, feeling rather hot and sick after the words I had listened to about being "hanged by the neck until I was dead," but still not caring much; for I could not rightly understand why all these fine gentlemen should be at the pains of Butchering me merely because I had run away from school (being so cruelly entreated by Gnawbit), and, to save myself from starvation, had joined the Blacks.

Being to Die, it seemed for the first time to occur to them that I was not as the rest of the poor souls that were doomed to death, and that it behoved them to treat me rather as a lamb that is doomed for the slaughter than as a great overgrown Bullock to be knocked down by the Butcher's Pole-axe. So they put me away from the rest of my companions, and bestowed me in a sorry little chamber, where I had a truckle-bed to myself. Dear old Mother Drum, being still under disgrace, was not suffered to come near me. Her trial, with that of Cicely Grip, for harbouring armed and disguised men, under the Black Act, which was likewise a felony, was not to come on till the next session. I believe that the Great Gentlemen at White-hall were, for a long time after my conviction, in a mind for Hanging me. 'Twas thought a small matter then to stretch the neck of a Boy of Twelve, and children even smaller than I had worn the white Nightcap, and smelt the Nosegay in the Cart. Indeed, I think the Ordinary wanted me to be Finished according to Law, that he might preach a Sermon on it, and liken me to one of the Children that mocked the Prophet, and was so eaten up by the She-Bears that came out of a Wood. When I think on the Reverend and Pious Persons who now attend our Criminals in their last unhappy Moments, and strive to bring them to a Sense of their Sins, it gives me the Goose-flesh to remember the Profane and Riotous Parsons who, for a Mean Stipend, did the contemned work of Gaol Chaplains in the days I speak of. Even while the Hangman was getting into proper Trim, and fashioning his tools for the slaughter, these callous Clergymen would be smoking and drinking with the keepers in the Lodge, talking now of a Main at Cocks and now of him who was to suffer on the Morrow, fleering and jesting, with the Church Service in one sleeve of their cassock and a Bottle Screw or a Pack of Cards in the other. And the Condemned persons, too, did not take the matter in a much more serious light. They had their Brandy and Tobacco even in their Dismal Hold, and thought much less of Mercy and Forgiveness than of the ease they would have from their Irons being stricken off, or the comfort they would gain from a last bellyful of Meat. I have not come to be sixty-eight years of age without observing somewhat of the Things that have passed around me; and one of the best signs of the Times in which I live (and due in great part to the Humane and Benignant complexion of his Majesty) is the falling off in bloodthirsty and cruel Punishments. If a Dozen or so are hanged after each Gaol Delivery at the Old Baily, and a score or more whipped or burnt in the Hand, what are such workings of justice compared with the Waste of Life that was used to be practised under the two last monarchs? At home 'twas all pressing to death those who would not plead, hanging, drawing, and quartering (how often have I sickened to see the pitch-seethed members of my Fellow-creatures on the spikes of Temple Bar and London Bridge!), taking out the entrails of those convict of Treason (as witness Colonel Towneley, Mr. Dawson, and many more unfortunate gentle-men on Kennington Common), to say nothing of the burning alive of women for petty treason,--and to kill a husband or coin a groat were alike Treasonable,--the Scourging of the same wretched creatures in Public till the blood ran from their shoulders and soaked the knots of the Beadle's lash; the cartings, brandings, and do-lorous Imprisonments which were then inflicted for the slightest of offences. Why, I have seen a man stand in the Pillory in the Seven Dials (to be certain, he was a secure scoundrel), and the Mob, not satisfied, must take him out, strip him to the buff, stone him, cast him down, root up the pillory, and trample him under foot, till, being Rescued by the constables, he has been taken back to Newgate, and has died in the Hackney Coach conveying him thither. Oh, 'tis woe to think of the Horrors that were then done in the name of the Law and Justice, not only in this country but in Foreign Parts,--with their Breakings on the Wheel, Questions Ordinary and Extraordinary, Bastinadoes, Carcans, Wooden horses, Burning alive too (for vend-ing of Irreligious Books), and the like Barbarities. Let me tell you likewise, that, for all the evil name gotten by the Spanish and Portuguese Inquisitions,--for which I entertain, as a Protestant, due Detestation and Abhorrence,--the darkest deeds ever done by the so called Holy Office in their Torture Chambers were not half so cruel as those performed with the full cognisance and approbation of authority, in open places, and in pursuance of the sentence of the Civil Judges. But a term has come to these wickednesses. The admirable Mr. Howard before named (whom I have often met in my travels, as he, good man, with nothing but a Biscuit and a few Raisins in his pocket, went up and down Europe Doing Good, smiling at Fever and tapping Pestilence on the cheek),--this Blessed Worthy has lightened the captive's fetters, and cleansed his dungeon, and given him Light and Air. Then I hear at the Coffee House that the great Judge, Sir William Blackstone, has given his caveat against the Frequency of Capital Punishment for small offences; and as His Majesty is notoriously averse from signing more than six Death Warrants at once (the old King used to say at council, in his German English, "Vere is de Dyin' speech man dat hang de Rogue for me?" meaning the Recorder with his Report, and seeming, in a sort, eager to despatch that awful Business, of which the present Prince is so Tender), I think that we have every cause to Bless the Times and Reign we live in. For surely 'tis but affected Softness of Heart, and Mock, Sickly Sentiment, to maintain that Highwaymen, Horse-stealers, and other hardened villains, do not deserve the Tree, and do not righteously Suffer for their misdeeds; or that wanton women do not deserve bodily correction, so long as it be done within Bridewell Walls, and not in front of the Sessions House, for the ribald Populace to stare at. Truly our present code is a merciful one, although I do not hold that the Extreme Penalty of the law should be exacted for such offences as cutting down growing trees, forging hat-stamps, or stealing above the value of a Shilling, or even of forty; nevertheless crime must be kept under, that is certain.[N]

At all events, they didn't hang John Dangerous. For a time, as I have said, the Great Gentlemen at Whitehall hesitated. I have heard that Justice Blackcap, being asked to intercede for me, did, with a scurril jest, tell Mr. Secretary that I was a young Imp of the Evil One, and that a little Hanging would do me no harm. Five, indeed, of my miserable companions were put to death, at different points on the borders of Charlwood Chase, and one, the unlucky Chaplain, met his fate before the door of the Stag o' Tyne. The rest of the Blacks, of whom, to my joy, I shall have no further occasion to speak, were sent to be Slaves in the American Plantations.

I had lain in Gaol more than a month after my Sentence, when Mr. Shapcott, a good Quaker Gentleman of the place (who had suffered much for Conscience' sake, and was very Pitifully inclined to all those who were in Affliction), began to take some interest in my unhappy Self; calling me a strayed Lamb, a brand to be snatched from the burning, and the like. And he, by the humane connivance of the Mayor and other Justices, was now permitted to have access unto me, and to conciliate the Keeper, Mrs. Macphilader, by money-presents, to treat me with some kindness. Also he brought me many Good Books, in thin paper covers; the which, although I could understand but very little of their Saving Truths, yet caused me to shed many Tears, more Sweet than Bitter, and to acknowledge, when taxed with it in a Soothing way, that my former Manner of Life had been most Wicked. But I should do this good man foul injustice, were I to let it stand that his benevolence to me was confined to books. He and (ever remembered) Mistress Shapcott, his Meek and Pious Partner, and his daughter, Wingrace Shapcott (a tall and straight young woman, as Beautiful as an Angel), were continually bringing me Comforts and Needments, both in Raiment and Food. It churns my Old Heart now to think of that Beautiful Girl, sitting beside me in my dank Prison Room, the tears streaming from her mild eyes, calling me by Endearing names, and ever and anon taking my hand in hers, and sinking on her knees to the sodden floor (with no thought of soiling her kirtle), while with profound Fervour she prayed for the conversion of errant Me. Sure there are Hearts of Gold among those Broadbrims and their fair strait-laced Daughters. Many a Merchant's Money-bags I have spared for the sake of Mr. Barzillai Shapcott (late of Aylesbury). Many a Fair Woman have I intermitted from my Furious Will in remembrance of the good that was shown me, in the old time, by that pale, strait-gowned Wingrace yonder, with her meek Face and welling Eyes. Of my deep and grievous Sins they told me enow, but they forbore to Terrify me with Frightful Images of Unforgiving Wrath; speaking to me of Forgiveness alway, rather than of Torment. And once, when I had gotten, through favour of the Keeper, Mr. Dredlincourt his book on Death (and had half frightened myself into fits by reading the Apparition of Mrs. Veal), these good people must needs take it from me, telling me that such strong meat was not fit for Babes, and gave me in its place a pretty little chap-book, called "Joy for Friendly Friends." But that I am old and battered, and black as a Guinea Negro with sins, I would go join the Quakers now. Never mind their broad-brims, and theeing and thouing. I tell you, man, that they have hearts as soft as toast-and-butter, and that they do more good in a day than my Lord Bishop (with his coach-horses, forsooth!) does in a year. And oh, the pleasure of devalising one of these Proud Prelates, as I--that is some of my Friends--have done scores of times!

Nothing would suit the good Shapcotts but that I should write in mine own hand a Petition to the King's Majesty. The Magistrates, who now began to take some interest in me, were for having it drawn up by their Town Clerk, and me only to put my Mark to it; for they would not give a poor little Hangdog of a Black any credit of Clergy. But being told that I could both read and write, after a Fashion, it was agreed that I was to have myself the scrivening of the Document; they giving me some Forms and Hints for beginning and ending, and bidding me con my Bible, and choose such texts as I thought bore on my Unhappy Condition. And after Great Endeavours and many painful days, and calling all my little Scholarship under my Grandmother, the kind old schoolmistress of Foubert's Passage, Gnawbit (burn him!), and Captain Night, I succeeded in producing the following. I give it word for word as I wrote it, having kept a copy; but I need not say that, as a Gentleman of Fortune, my Style and Spelling are not now so Barbarous and Uncouth.

This was my Petition to His Majesty:

> "The Humble Pettyshon of Jon Dangerous now a prisinner
>   under centense off Deth in His Maggesty's Gayle at
>   Alesbury to his Maggesty Gorge by the grease of God
>   King of Grate Briton Frans and Eyearland Deffender
>   off the Fathe Showeth That yore Petetioner which I
>   am Unfortunate enuff to be mixed up in this
>   business Me and the others wich have suffered was
>   Cast by the Jewry and Justis Blackcapp he ses that
>   as a Warming and Eggsample i am to be Hanged by the
>   Nek till you are Ded and the Lord have Mercy upon
>   his Soul Great Sur your Maggesty the Book ses that
>   wen the wicked man turneth away from his Wickedness
>   wich he have committed and doeth that wich is
>   Lawful and Rite he shall save his Sole alive
>   Therefore deer Great Sur wich a repreive would fall
>   like Thunder upon a Contrite Hart and am most

sorrowful under the Black Act wich it is true I
took the deere but was led to it Deere Sur wich
Mungo and others was repreeved at the Tree and sent
to the Plantations but am not twelve yeeres old And
have always been a Prottestant Great Sur i shall be
happy to serve his Maggesty by see or land and if
the Grannydeere he had not Vexed me but had no
other way being in a Korner and all Fiting and so i
up with the demmyjon which i hoap he is better And
your Petishioner will ever pray your Maggesty's
loving Subject and Servant

JON DANGEROUS.

My Granmother was a Lady of Quality and lived in
her own House in Hannover Squair and was used after
her Deth very cruelly by one Mistress Tallmash and
Kadwallader which was the Stoard and was sent in a
Waggin like a Beggar Deere Sur Mr. Gnawbit he used
me shameful wich I was Blak and Blue and the Old
Gentleman he ses you Run away ses he into Charwood
chaise and join the Blaks Deere Sur this is All
which Captain Nite would sware but as eloped I am
now lying here many weekes Deere Sur I shood like
to be hanged in Wite for I am Innocent leastways of
meaning to kill the Grannydeere."

This was a Curious kind of Schoolboy letter. Different I take it from those one
gets from a Brother, asking for a Crown, a Pony, or a Plumcake. But my Schools had
been of the hardest, and this was *my* Holiday letter.

When the Mayor read it, he burst out a-laughing, and says that no such Thieves'
Flash must be sent to the Foot of the Throne. But Mr. Shapcott told him that he
would not have one word altered; that he would not even strike out the paragraph

where I had been irreverent enough to quote a Text (and spell it badly); and that what I had written, and naught else, should go to the King. He took it to London himself, and his Majesty being much elated by some successes in Germany, and the Discovery of a Jacobite Plot, and moved moreover by the intercession of a Foreign Lady, that was his favourite, and who vowed that the little Deer-Stealer's Petition was Monstrous Droll, and almost as good as a Play,--His Majesty was graciously pleased to remit my Sentence, on condition of my transporting myself for life to His Majesty's Plantations in North America.

As to my transporting "myself," that was a Fiction. I was henceforth as much a Slave to my own Countrymen as I was in after days to the Moors. The Shapcotts would willingly have provided me with the means of going to the uttermost ends of the World, but that was not the way the thing was to be done. Flesh and Blood were bought and sold in those days, and it did not much matter about the colour. By that strange Laxity which then tempered the severity of the Laws, I was permitted, for many days after my Fate was settled, to remain in a kind of semi-Enlargement. I suppose that Mr. Shapcott gave bail for me; but I was taken into his Family, and treated with the most Loving Kindness, till the fearful intelligence came that I, with two hundred other Convicts, had been "Taken up" for Transportation by Sir Basil Hopwood, a rich Merchant and Alderman of London, who paid a certain Sum a head for us to the King's Government for taking us to America, where he might make what profit he pleased, by selling our wretched Carcasses to be Slaves to the Planters.

Oh, the terrible Parting! but there was no other Way, and it had to be Endured. My kind friends made me up a packet of Necessaries for the Voyage, and with a Heavy Heart I bade them farewell. These good people are all Dead; but their woman-servant, Ruth, a pure soul, of great Serenity of Countenance, still lives; and every Christmas does the Carrier convey for me to Aylesbury a Hamper full of the Good Things of this Life, and Ten Golden Guineas. And I know that this Good and Faithful Servant (who has been well provided for) just touches the Kissing-crust of one of the Pies my Lilias has made for her, and that she goes straight with the rest, Money and Cates, to the Gaol, and therewith relieves the Debtors (whom Heaven deliver out of their Captivity!). And it is more seemly that she rather than I should do this thing, seeing that there are those who will not believe that after a Hard Life a man can keep a fleshy heart, and who would be apt to dub me Hypocrite if these Doles came from me directly.

NOTE:

[N] Captain Dangerous, it will be seen, was, in regard to our criminal code, somewhat in advance of the ideas of his age, but he was scarcely on a level with those of our own, and, I think, would have perused with some surprise the speeches of Mr. Ewart and the *Vacation Thoughts on Capital Punishments* of the late Mr. Commissioner Phillips.--ED.

The Codes Of Hammurabi And Moses
W. W. Davies

QTY

The discovery of the Hammurabi Code is one of the greatest achievements of archaeology, and is of paramount interest, not only to the student of the Bible, but also to all those interested in ancient history...

Religion   **ISBN:** *1-59462-338-4*   **Pages:**132

MSRP $12.95

The Theory of Moral Sentiments
Adam Smith

QTY

This work from 1749. contains original theories of conscience amd moral judgment and it is the foundation for systemof morals.

Philosophy ISBN: *1-59462-777-0*   **Pages:**536

MSRP $19.95

Jessica's First Prayer
Hesba Stretton

QTY

In a screened and secluded corner of one of the many railway-bridges which span the streets of London there could be seen a few years ago, from five o'clock every morning until half past eight, a tidily set-out coffee-stall, consisting of a trestle and board, upon which stood two large tin cans, with a small fire of charcoal burning under each so as to keep the coffee boiling during the early hours of the morning when the work-people were thronging into the city on their way to their daily toil...

Pages:84

Childrens   ISBN: *1-59462-373-2*   *MSRP $9.95*

My Life and Work
Henry Ford

QTY

Henry Ford revolutionized the world with his implementation of mass production for the Model T automobile. Gain valuable business insight into his life and work with his own auto-biography... "We have only started on our development of our country we have not as yet, with all our talk of wonderful progress, done more than scratch the surface. The progress has been wonderful enough but..."

Pages:300

Biographies/   ISBN: *1-59462-198-5*   *MSRP $21.95*

The Art of Cross-Examination
Francis Wellman

QTY

I presume it is the experience of every author, after his first book is published upon an important subject, to be almost overwhelmed with a wealth of ideas and illustrations which could readily have been included in his book, and which to his own mind, at least, seem to make a second edition inevitable. Such certainly was the case with me; and when the first edition had reached its sixth impression in five months, I rejoiced to learn that it seemed to my publishers that the book had met with a sufficiently favorable reception to justify a second and considerably enlarged edition. ..

Pages:412

Reference   **ISBN: *1-59462-647-2***   *MSRP $19.95*

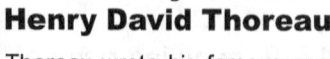

On the Duty of Civil Disobedience
Henry David Thoreau

QTY

Thoreau wrote his famous essay, On the Duty of Civil Disobedience, as a protest against an unjust but popular war and the immoral but popular institution of slave-owning. He did more than write—he declined to pay his taxes, and was hauled off to gaol in consequence. Who can say how much this refusal of his hastened the end of the war and of slavery ?

Law   **ISBN: *1-59462-747-9***   **Pages:48**

MSRP $7.45

Dream Psychology Psychoanalysis for Beginners
Sigmund Freud

QTY

Sigmund Freud, born Sigismund Schlomo Freud (May 6, 1856 - September 23, 1939), was a Jewish-Austrian neurologist and psychiatrist who co-founded the psychoanalytic school of psychology. Freud is best known for his theories of the unconscious mind, especially involving the mechanism of repression; his redefinition of sexual desire as mobile and directed towards a wide variety of objects; and his therapeutic techniques, especially his understanding of transference in the therapeutic relationship and the presumed value of dreams as sources of insight into unconscious desires.

Pages:196

Psychology   **ISBN: *1-59462-905-6***   *MSRP $15.45*

The Miracle of Right Thought
Orison Swett Marden

QTY

Believe with all of your heart that you will do what you were made to do. When the mind has once formed the habit of holding cheerful, happy, prosperous pictures, it will not be easy to form the opposite habit. It does not matter how improbable or how far away this realization may see, or how dark the prospects may be, if we visualize them as best we can, as vividly as possible, hold tenaciously to them and vigorously struggle to attain them, they will gradually become actualized, realized in the life. But a desire, a longing without endeavor, a yearning abandoned or held indifferently will vanish without realization.

Pages:360

Self Help   **ISBN: *1-59462-644-8***   *MSRP $25.45* www.bookjungle.com *email: sales@bookjungle.com fax: 630-214-0564 mail: Book Jungle PO Box 2226 Champaign, IL 61825*

QTY

The Rosicrucian Cosmo-Conception Mystic Christianity *by Max Heindel* ISBN: *1-59462-188-8* **$38.95**
The Rosicrucian Cosmo-conception is not dogmatic, neither does it appeal to any other authority than the reason of the student. It is: not controversial, but is: sent forth in the, hope that it may help to clear... New Age/Religion Pages 646

Abandonment To Divine Providence *by Jean-Pierre de Caussade* ISBN: *1-59462-228-0* **$25.95**
"The Rev. Jean Pierre de Caussade was one of the most remarkable spiritual writers of the Society of Jesus in France in the 18th Century. His death took place at Toulouse in 1751. His works have gone through many editions and have been republished... Inspirational/Religion Pages 400

Mental Chemistry *by Charles Haanel* ISBN: *1-59462-192-6* **$23.95**
Mental Chemistry allows the change of material conditions by combining and appropriately utilizing the power of the mind. Much like applied chemistry creates something new and unique out of careful combinations of chemicals the mastery of mental chemistry... New Age Pages 354

The Letters of Robert Browning and Elizabeth Barret Barrett 1845-1846 vol II ISBN: *1-59462-193-4* **$35.95**
by Robert Browning and Elizabeth Barrett Biographies Pages 596

Gleanings In Genesis (volume I) *by Arthur W. Pink* ISBN: *1-59462-130-6* **$27.45**
Appropriately has Genesis been termed "the seed plot of the Bible" for in it we have, in germ form, almost all of the great doctrines which are afterwards fully developed in the books of Scripture which follow... Religion/Inspirational Pages 420

The Master Key *by L. W. de Laurence* ISBN: *1-59462-001-6* **$30.95**
In no branch of human knowledge has there been a more lively increase of the spirit of research during the past few years than in the study of Psychology, Concentration and Mental Discipline. The requests for authentic lessons in Thought Control, Mental Discipline and... New Age/Business Pages 422

The Lesser Key Of Solomon Goetia *by L. W. de Laurence* ISBN: *1-59462-092-X* **$9.95**
This translation of the first book of the "Lemegton" which is now for the first time made accessible to students of Talismanic Magic was done, after careful collation and edition, from numerous Ancient Manuscripts in Hebrew, Latin, and French... New Age/Occult Pages 92

Rubaiyat Of Omar Khayyam *by Edward Fitzgerald* ISBN:*1-59462-332-5* **$13.95**
Edward Fitzgerald, whom the world has already learned, in spite of his own efforts to remain within the shadow of anonymity, to look upon as one of the rarest poets of the century, was born at Bredfield, in Suffolk, on the 31st of March, 1809. He was the third son of John Purcell... Music Pages 172

Ancient Law *by Henry Maine* ISBN: *1-59462-128-4* **$29.95**
The chief object of the following pages is to indicate some of the earliest ideas of mankind, as they are reflected in Ancient Law, and to point out the relation of those ideas to modern thought. Religiom/History Pages 452

Far-Away Stories *by William J. Locke* ISBN: *1-59462-129-2* **$19.45**
"Good wine needs no bush, but a collection of mixed vintages does. And this book is just such a collection. Some of the stories I do not want to remain buried for ever in the museum files of dead magazine-numbers an author's not unpardonable vanity..." Fiction Pages 272

Life of David Crockett *by David Crockett* ISBN: *1-59462-250-7* **$27.45**
"Colonel David Crockett was one of the most remarkable men of the times in which he lived. Born in humble life, but gifted with a strong will, an indomitable courage, and unremitting perseverance... Biographies/New Age Pages 424

Lip-Reading *by Edward Nitchie* ISBN: *1-59462-206-X* **$25.95**
Edward B. Nitchie, founder of the New York School for the Hard of Hearing, now the Nitchie School of Lip-Reading, Inc, wrote "LIP-READING Principles and Practice". The development and perfecting of this meritorious work on lip-reading was an undertaking... How-to Pages 400

A Handbook of Suggestive Therapeutics, Applied Hypnotism, Psychic Science ISBN: *1-59462-214-0* **$24.95**
by Henry Munro Health/New Age/Health/Self-help Pages 376

A Doll's House: and Two Other Plays *by Henrik Ibsen* ISBN: *1-59462-112-8* **$19.95**
Henrik Ibsen created this classic when in revolutionary 1848 Rome. Introducing some striking concepts in playwriting for the realist genre, this play has been studied the world over. Fiction/Classics/Plays 308

The Light of Asia *by sir Edwin Arnold* ISBN: *1-59462-204-3* **$13.95**
In this poetic masterpiece, Edwin Arnold describes the life and teachings of Buddha. The man who was to become known as Buddha to the world was born as Prince Gautama of India but he rejected the worldly riches and abandoned the reigns of power when... Religion/History/Biographies Pages 170

The Complete Works of Guy de Maupassant *by Guy de Maupassant* ISBN: *1-59462-157-8* **$16.95**
"For days and days, nights and nights, I had dreamed of that first kiss which was to consecrate our engagement, and I knew not on what spot I should put my lips..." Fiction/Classics Pages 240

The Art of Cross-Examination *by Francis L. Wellman* ISBN: *1-59462-309-0* **$26.95**
Written by a renowned trial lawyer, Wellman imparts his experience and uses case studies to explain how to use psychology to extract desired information through questioning. How-to/Science/Reference Pages 408

Answered or Unanswered? *by Louisa Vaughan* ISBN: *1-59462-248-5* **$10.95**
Miracles of Faith in China Religion Pages 112

The Edinburgh Lectures on Mental Science (1909) *by Thomas* ISBN: *1-59462-008-3* **$11.95**
This book contains the substance of a course of lectures recently given by the writer in the Queen Street Hail, Edinburgh. Its purpose is to indicate the Natural Principles governing the relation between Mental Action and Material Conditions... New Age/Psychology Pages 148

Ayesha *by H. Rider Haggard* ISBN: *1-59462-301-5* **$24.95**
Verily and indeed it is the unexpected that happens! Probably if there was one person upon the earth from whom the Editor of this, and of a certain previous history, did not expect to hear again... Classics Pages 380

Ayala's Angel *by Anthony Trollope* ISBN: *1-59462-352-X* **$29.95**
The two girls were both pretty, but Lucy who was twenty-one who supposed to be simple and comparatively unattractive, whereas Ayala was credited, as her Bombwhat romantic name might show, with poetic charm and a taste for romance. Ayala when her father died was nineteen... Fiction Pages 484

The American Commonwealth *by James Bryce* ISBN: *1-59462-286-8* **$34.45**
An interpretation of American democratic political theory. It examines political mechanics and society from the perspective of Scotsman James Bryce Politics Pages 572

Stories of the Pilgrims *by Margaret P. Pumphrey* ISBN: *1-59462-116-0* **$17.95**
This book explores pilgrims religious oppression in England as well as their escape to Holland and eventual crossing to America on the Mayflower, and their early days in New England... History Pages 268

QTY

The Fasting Cure *by Sinclair Upton*   ISBN: *1-59462-222-1* **$13.95**
In the Cosmopolitan Magazine for May, 1910, and in the Contemporary Review (London) for April, 1910, I published an article dealing with my experiences in fasting. I have written a great many magazine articles, but never one which attracted so much attention... New Age/Self Help/Health Pages 164

Hebrew Astrology *by Sepharial*   ISBN: *1-59462-308-2* **$13.45**
In these days of advanced thinking it is a matter of common observation that we have left many of the old landmarks behind and that we are now pressing forward to greater heights and to a wider horizon than that which represented the mind-content of our progenitors... Astrology Pages 144

Thought Vibration or The Law of Attraction in the Thought World   ISBN: *1-59462-127-6* **$12.95**
by William Walker Atkinson   Psychology/Religion Pages 144

Optimism *by Helen Keller*   ISBN: *1-59462-108-X* **$15.95**
Helen Keller was blind, deaf, and mute since 19 months old, yet famously learned how to overcome these handicaps, communicate with the world, and spread her lectures promoting optimism. An inspiring read for everyone... Biographies/Inspirational Pages 84

Sara Crewe *by Frances Burnett*   ISBN: *1-59462-360-0* **$9.45**
In the first place, Miss Minchin lived in London. Her home was a large, dull, tall one, in a large, dull square, where all the houses were alike, and all the sparrows were alike, and where all the door-knockers made the same heavy sound... Childrens/Classic Pages 88

The Autobiography of Benjamin Franklin *by Benjamin Franklin*   ISBN: *1-59462-135-7* **$24.95**
The Autobiography of Benjamin Franklin has probably been more extensively read than any other American historical work, and no other book of its kind has had such ups and downs of fortune. Franklin lived for many years in England, where he was agent... Biographies/History Pages 332

Name	
Email	
Telephone	
Address	
City, State ZIP	

☐ **Credit Card**   ☐ **Check / Money Order**

Credit Card Number	
Expiration Date	
Signature	

Please Mail to: Book Jungle
                   PO Box 2226
                   Champaign, IL 61825
or Fax to: 630-214-0564